THE INVASION OF NORMANDIE

A Novel of Celebrity

JEFF POLMAN

Grassy Gutter Press
Culver City, CA

ALSO BY THE AUTHOR

1924 and You Are There!
Ball Nuts
Mystery Ball '58
Twinbill

Cover design by the author
Author photo by Carmen Patti

for Marilyn and Rebecca

PROLOGUE:
WEST HOLLYWOOD

Deep in the dressing room of Toxic Gecko, an expensive European boutique on Melrose Avenue owned by a world-famous Slavic fashion designer, Normandie Vine was staring at herself in the mirror.

This in itself was nothing new. Normandie had been staring at herself in mirrors for so long she was starting to believe she lived inside them. Not like Alice through her looking-glass, though. That was fun, Victorian, and somewhat psychedelic. More like a homeless woman downtown off Figueroa, gazing into the glass window of an abandoned loan company, or an oily puddle in the gutter, and wondering who she was exactly looking at.

On the surface, Normandie's appearance hadn't changed since her *Berserk Love* album broke the *Billboard* charts back in '09. She was garbed in absurdly tight black leather pants, with a scarlet bra visible beneath a see-through creamy top. An explosion of red hair crowned an angelic face and large, hypnotic eyes. She was pushing thirty and the eyes were often bloodshot these days but hell, she was still razor cute and knew how to flaunt it. As her agent/publicist/manager/surrogate mother Myra Harp once coined, if you blended a talented little match girl with a Russian hooker, you'd get Normandie Vine, and the concoction had helped make her financially comfortable for over a decade.

There were those other things in her life, though. The ones that surfaced every day and either poked at her ribs, crawled up her spine, or smacked her silly. Such as the fans stalking her every time she crossed a parking lot, the young employees pestering her at Sprouts or Amoeba Music, or the five times revealing photos of her at 19 had been posted on the Internet in the last year. Yes, she had chosen the worlds of acting and popular music long ago and they came with this nonsense, but the cesspool had become so vast and so deep she was wondering all over again what it was really for.

"Ms. Vine? How you are coming?" Anichka's Ukranian accent peppered the dressing room door from the other side.

"Just fine…" was Normandie's muted, obligatory answer. "Five more minutes, okay?" The thousand dollar ripped skinny jeans by Skull Montez that Anichka had asked her to "consider please" were still draped across the little stool beside the mirror. Per usual, she was going to buy the pants without trying them on. If she couldn't get into them at home later, Chuck or Rashid would just return them for her and secure a huge store credit.

* * *

Outside Toxic Gecko, at the corner of Melrose and Stanley, a weathered mini-van pulled up to the corner and double parked. A side door rolled open, and Monty Matilda hopped onto the curb in a grey nimbus cloud of cigar smoke. Two hundred and seventy-five pounds of Brisbane ruddiness, the ex-Australian rules football star turned celebrity photographer had the curly ginger hair of a madman and the eyes of a hungry condor. Two 35mm cameras, four lenses and a string of film canisters were slung over his hulking shoulder like Gatling gun bullets. He paused on the sidewalk and instantly noted the drawn blinds of the store, the gathering pedestrians, and especially the two other double-parked vehicles of photographers, their front and back doors wide open, shadowy figures within braced for a Normandie exit.

"Shit on a cracker," he muttered.

* * *

In the dressing room, Normandie spooned some cocaine into an open plastic bottle of papaya juice, then dug into her bag, fished out two tiny Aeromexico bottles of tequila and added them to the juice. She stared into her creation for a few seconds, then stuck her thumb on top, shook the hell out of the thing and swallowed it down.

"Ms. Vine? Hello??"

Her body quivered. She bent forward, took some deep breaths. "Yeah, yeah. Coming!" she cried, then quickly assembled her belongings and unlocked the dressing room door.

Anichka's white face and exploding smile were jarring. Behind her, a half dozen young Toxic Gecko employees waited for further direction. There were no other customers in the store.

"Jeans fit good?"

"Huh? Oh—yeah..." She ducked back in and scooped them off the stool after a few failed attempts. "I'll take these, and those two blouses I liked before." She dropped the pants in Anichka's arms and drifted toward the register in the middle of the store. They were blasting Nomandie's latest hip-hoppish number "Baby Makes Me Wanna" over the store speakers, and in her brain haze she could still make out a few excited squeals from the sidewalk. Through the slats in the store's blinds, young eyeballs peered.

A humorless salesgirl sporting an eyebrow ring began ringing up Normandie's clothes. Normandie leaned on the counter to keep from falling and gazed at her with a sad, almost mesmerized expression.

"I love how you do that..."

"Huh?" replied the salesgirl.

"The way you do your job. You're so professional...so calm."

Anichka stuck her face between them. Normandie tried not to look at it. "Will there be anything else, Ms.—"

"No! I mean—not this time. Thanks, Anichka."

"Okay!" said the salesgirl, "Your total today comes to two thousand and twenty-four dollars and 59 cents."

"We will call that two thousand even, no?" offered Anichka.

"Sounds cool to me. Just use my tab..." Normandie continued to stare at the salesgirl as she quickly bagged up the clothes, noting the girl's name tag that said KRISTIN. The second she dropped in the sales receipt, Normandie leaned in and lowered her voice to a drowsy whisper.

"Hey, Kristin. Do you have any openings?"

"What's that?"

"I would be good at this. Seriously. Show up on time and everything. People really like me—you know, when I'm not performing."

The girl recoiled. Anichka wordlessly slid between them one more time, handed Normandie her bag and guided her away from the counter. The moment Normandie turned, the entire store jolted to life as if a power line had dropped through the roof. Employees whispered into little headsets, rolled clothing racks aside, carved out a human path to the rear exit door in seconds. Normandie fished out her Bulgari sunglasses and glided into the sharp Autumn sunlight in her newest dream state.

Monty Matilda studied the alley. Delbert, his young, nearly mute assistant, had parked the van in a large slice of shade across Stanley with ample room to pull off a U-turn. The moment Monty spotted Normandie's cloudburst of hair emerge from Toxic Gecko's back door, he crackled a smile and tossed his cigar in the gutter.

"Start the motor, Delbie."

Normandie wobbled to her teel blue Benz convertible. A half dozen empty Tasmanian Rain water bottles littered the back seat. She plopped behind the wheel, and something in her field of blurry vision caught her eye. Reached around and plucked a piece of note paper from under the windshield wiper. Read its scrawled words:

EVERY BREATH YOU TAKE, LUV...

Across the street, Monty saw Normandie crumple the note in her hand. His entire face glowed.

"I'll be watching you..."

Normandie revved the Benz's motor. Monty hooted and slapped Delbert's arm. The van lurched across Stanley, gunned up the alley behind her. Normandie's Benz screeched out the far end, hooked left, peeled around the corner onto Melrose and nearly hit three pedestrians. Delbert went straight, kept the van in the alley, Monty's eyes tracking every visible sliver of Melrose.

Normandie swerved the Benz through traffic, pumping the gas and brake like a Monte Carlo finalist. Glanced in her rear view mirror, saw no Monty and beamed with delight.

"EAT ME, MATE!"

The red light at Fairfax was just ahead, cars backed up. Normandie slowed, then saw Monty's van lurch out of an alley on the right, just twenty yards ahead. She slammed the brakes, shoved the Benz into reverse, crunching a bumper behind her. Horns and curses erupted. She put the car back in drive, wheeled around three cars and jumped the light—

Witnesses would later recall the LAPD cruiser traveling at about 35 miles an hour. The sound its front bumper made when it smashed into the right side of Normandie's Benz, spun her car around twice and knocked it into a bus shelter was like a glass and metal bomb, shattering the crisp October day and plunging its driver into an even deeper darkness than she was used to.

CHAPTER ONE:
POPLAR AVENUE

Ten miles north of Nebraska Interstate 80 lay the town of
Endeavor, a place so insignificant that if migrating geese
could talk even *they* would be calling it "flyover country". Oh, it did
have a Main Street, but that was only two blocks long and half of
the buildings were shuttered. Tip Top Feed had moved out to the
Route 80A business route two years earlier, and Rita's Hot Tacos
was threatening to. No one had bothered to take down the old Tip
Top sign or find a new occupant, and tall prairie weeds had helped
themselves to the real estate.

The population of Endeavor was 923, or "close to a thousand!"
as lone Chamber of Commerce employee Dot Rutherford liked
to tell people in the hopeful emails she sent out blindly every few
months to try and lure businesses from Omaha. Most of the town's
inhabitants were corn farmers or uranium miners, but many were
unemployed and living on government checks, or lucky enough to
work at the handful of other Endeavor establishments that were
still operating: Jerry's Gas, Butchie's Hardware, Googy's Market,
the Endeavor Animal Clinic, and the town's only coffee house, the
Lonesome Drip—two tables and a big Keurig machine wedged
inside an abandoned boot shop.

There were about ten square blocks of houses in town, a
smattering of them being trailers, though nearly every residence
sported a satellite dish. There was a tiny Endeavor Library and one
public school covering grades K through 12. Endeavor Square was
the name of the rectangular block of parched grass, bench, scary
water fountain, and two ancient Cottonwoods that served as the town
"park". Police Chief Tim Gilmore spent most of his summer hours
chasing beer-drinking teens and the occasional meth head out of it.

The largest grade 9 through 12 class at Bill Baird School had about eleven students, and the only athletics it could afford was a touch football team called the Galloping Huskers, which competed every Saturday in the South Central Nebraska Touch League against three other sparsely-budgeted towns.

As in most high schools, there were cliques and perennially bored kids, but Bill Baird had one thing going for it that other facilities in Endeavor lacked: excellent wi-fi. It was perched on a small rise alongside an abandoned sand and gravel mine, and angled so that it directly faced a 200-ft-high cell tower five miles away that Chickesaw County had constructed to aid passing truckers.

Fran Dunwoody loved the wi-fi.

She had heard stories from Uncle Dave about life in the early '80s, when there was no Internet yet and people got these things called "busy signals" sometimes when they tried to call someone, but that concept was almost hard to believe. All she knew was that the wi-fi made algebra class bearable. Fran was awful smart for a 14-year-old, but algebra was less exciting to her than dog spit. Come to think of it, few subjects beat dog spit, other than maybe world history when they brought up Joan of Arc or the Black Plague.

Anyway, on the first Friday in November, with high chilly winds blowing down from Manitoba and rattling the window hinges in the classroom, Fran dropped her gaze back to her iPhone the second Ms. Mendez turned her head to explain a new incomprehensible equation she had just written on the blackboard.

And that was when she saw the breaking news item:

NORMANDIE VINE TO REHAB IN COLORADO

Fran's sun-deprived face flushed. Her red-dyed spiky hair felt like it was going to ignite. Yeah, Celebofizz was a cheesy, sensational, often inaccurate Website, but their app never crashed and they carried more Normandie news than anyone. She scrolled down with a thumb and devoured every word. Glanced up at Ms. Mendez one more time, then quickly fired off a two-thumb text to her sister.

* * *

The school joke was that short, stocky Fran and tall, skittish Trish came from two different mailmen. They didn't mind the crack; at least it was attention. Trish was playing the coronet to "Stayin' Alive" in band class when the phone in her skirt pocket throbbed. She never cared for the Bee Gees much, and the Bill Baird Band had no real football team to perform in front of, but like her late dad and mom—and of course Uncle Dave—she enjoyed music a lot, playing and singing along to classic rock radio, making an occasional video of herself, and having designs on someday being a lead vocalist in a popular bar band, headlining in small towns up and down the Missouri with cover versions of Cranberries songs or even oldies like Bon Jovi.

What the heck did Fran want now? Nobody but her bossy younger sister ever texted her, and nutty Uncle Dave was still a year away from breaking down and learning how to send one. She suffered her way through the final bars of the song, then dug out her phone while Mr. Hornglass announced a five-minute break. Fran had linked to the Celebofizz page, and typed four words: MT. GARBAGE BEFORE LUNCH!

Trish jabbed the link. Read about four sentences of the story before the coronet fell off her lap and clattered across the floor.

* * *

Mt. Garbage was what Bill Baird students called a monolithic iron dumpster parked around the side of the school. The thing was so ancient it may have once contained Pawnee feathers, and now doubled as a depository for fast food wrappers, broken desks, and old homework. Due to its rusty girth and ability to shield students from both school windows and prairie winds, it was also a prime cigarette-sneaking spot and meeting place for any kind of clandestine reason. Freshmen knew enough to stay clear.

Fran was pacing alongside Mt. Garbage and looked up to see Trish, zipping up her pink hoodie and looking concerned already.

"Colorado seems so wrong for her. I mean, I can see Big Sur

again, maybe even Palm Desert, except the last retreat there wasn't exactly—"

"Whaddya think?" interrupted Fran.

"What do I think about what?"

"Operation Support!"

"You don't mean..." Trish turned even more pale than usual. "But we haven't started Old Jeannie in like a month—"

"SSH!"

Trish glanced left. The Cookie Monsters—Cookie Calhoun, Heather, Irene, and Lakota—were strolling by Mt. Garbage. Each girl was more catty, loudly dressed, and incomprehensibly popular than the next. Trish liked to call them the I.P.S. (Invaders from Planet Shallow), but Fran had settled on the Cookie Monsters. They despised them for many reasons, but the time they organized a protest for not being able to pose with their guns in the school yearbook had been the icing on the despicable cake. They sneered in Trish and Fran's general direction, but thankfully kept moving.

"Anyway," resumed Trish, her voice a notch lower, "Uncle Dave will freak. Out."

"Not if he doesn't know. And if we get our homework done by Sunday night. We got the whole weekend here."

Trish kicked at a small pile of cigarette butts fossilized in the hard dirt at her feet. "This Colorado place can only be good for her, right?"

"Normandie totaled a freakin' police car, Trish. Anything but a jail cell would be good for her."

"Should we tell Dana?"

"Oh no. He will geek out way too much. Either way we should try and get him over tonight to help us."

"Help us with what?"

"Whaddya think? The operation!"

* * *

Dave Dunwoody was having a tough time again. The nurse had inserted the IV in Gumdrop's paw and the shot of Xylazine was ready in Dave's hand, but crouching in front of the skeletal orange tabby that was nestled in her weeping owner's arms, he just couldn't bring himself to inject the drug.

"She was a rescue kitty," said Mara Pelt from inside her grey bangs. "Sweet as all get-out, never complained—"

"Yes. Yes, I can see that. Now are you sure you're comfortable with this?"

Mara was slightly taken aback. "Why...of course! Isn't that why I'm here?"

"Right. Exactly. It's just that this is a big decision for a lot of people, and we just like to be certain—"

"I'm ready, Dr. Dunwoody. We both are."

She gave Gumdrop a final loving squeeze. Dave took a deep breath. The "sleep room" where the Endeavor Animal Clinic conducted its euthanasia had purposely dim lighting, a soft couch for pets and their owners, and bad new age music playing on a loop. Dave removed his thick round glasses for a moment and wiped a speck of dust out of the corner of his eye. Although he had turned 35 two weeks ago and wrinkly remnants of his endless party days cupped his eyes, he still had his boyish good looks. On the other hand, he'd had a number of hesitant moments like this in the past year, and was starting to worry about them. Dave knew he was a good veternarian, and had a framed diploma from Nebraska College of Technical Agriculture in Curtis to remind him, but at the moment, the diploma was down the hall in his office.

"Doctor?"

He bit his lip and inserted the Xylazine in the IV.

"The first drug is a strong sedative to relax her. The second is a barbiturate that will..." He gave a little shrug. "You know..."

He felt around in his lab coat for the second shot. Even in the dim light he could see tears drip and glisten on Mara's cheek.

"You doing okay?"

"Mm-hmm."

The cat went completely limp in her arms. Mara's mouth clenched. She wanted to wail but managed to restrain herself. Dave's right hand began to shake, though, and he had a hard time inserting the second needle into the IV.

"Dang..."

He finally stood up, went to the door and opened it a crack.

"Patty? Need your help."

Patty, his mid-20s nurse/receptionist with a serious weight problem and monster crush on her boss, came down the hall. She knew right away what he needed and took the syringe from him.

"Sure, Dr. Dunwoody. Any time."

* * *

A pink sky painted the west when Dave climbed into his grey 15-year-old Volvo with the crack in the side mirror and drank an entire can of Coke Zero while the engine warmed. He popped on his home-burned CD of 39 vintage country-western tunes that perpetually played in his car. "Forgive Me One More Time" by Spade Cooley and the Western Swing Dance Gang came on, calming him in seconds, and he was ready to drive.

It was less than ten minutes home, but the route always seemed to take longer because it passed through Endeavor Center. A crawling tractor or long grain truck would invariably slow down a handful of cars, giving Fred Gibbons a chance to step off his usual corner at Main and Oak, approach Dave's window and ask how the family was doing. This was a block away from where Dot Rutherford always emerged from the Chamber of Commerce, waved at Dave's car from the sidewalk and asked with a yell how the family was doing. If Chief Gilmore happened to be in the street waving traffic around the stalled grain truck, it was difficult for Dave to go by without beating him to the punch and rolling down his window to let *him* know how the family was doing. Of course, Dave would also give every motorist he passed on the way home a customary two-finger salute off the steering wheel, an act that took no time at all but because it involved Dave briefly pausing to size up who the person was, seemed to. Despite two gaping holes in his life, being instinctively friendly was still in Dave's bones.

Dave's Volvo knew the way home rather well, and practically

slowed down by itself a few blocks past the heart of Main Street. "Dark Eyes Dance" by the original Light Crust Doughboys was playing, and his left leg bounced. He slowed to five miles an hour at a flashing yellow light, just to be extra careful, then rounded the corner and turned right onto Poplar Avenue.

For years and years in the 1800s, Burnt Willow was the name of the town, until a retired railroad baron with a desire for tranquility named Delbert Boggs moved there, became the mayor, sparked a surge in prosperity and built an entire street of quaint little Victorian dwellings to match the style of his much larger one at the end of the block. To set the street off from the rest of the town he planted two rows of poplar trees and invited a handful of cronies from his railroad days to inhabit most of the homes. When Boggs died in a drowning accident over in Lake McConaughy in 1921, his wife left with the children, the house burned down in a semi-suspicious fire and the spirit and optimism he had brought to the town he had since renamed Endeavor largely vanished. But Poplar Avenue remained.

The street was a local curiosity that its residents always felt some pride in. Christmas lights were more extravagant, and more than a few Endeavorites from "down the hill" spent a December Sunday evening or two cruising up and down the block to take them in. No Endeavor neighborhood was more crowded with trick-or-treaters on Halloween. The lot at the far end where the Boggs house stood was now a giant fenced-off briar patch, but the wire fence was open in two places, and many local kids had used the few blackened areas and crumbled stone remnants of the house's foundation as sort of an auxiliary Mt. Garbage.

Dave always slowed his Volvo to a crawl when he turned onto Poplar, partly to eye the neighbor's lawns, partly out of sheer reverence. The Dunwoody house was the third one on the left, number 12, its front yard leaves now cleanly raked for the fourth or fifth time—with begrudging help from Trish and Fran, of course—and it was still, Dave felt, the sweetest-looking home on Poplar Avenue. Like the others, it was only one story, but his sister-in-law Jean had painted it a bright canary yellow with forest green shutters

and door, and a Victorian wraparound porch with Queen Anne
lace made the structure seem fancier than it was. The house was
also perched on a little rise, the only piece of ground on Poplar that
had one, giving the lot a slight regal quality Dave never failed to feel
guilty about.

It wasn't the only thing he felt guilty about. Aching sadness always
enveloped Dave at this climax of the drive, because 12 Poplar Avenue
wasn't really his house.

The summer morning over ten years ago when he promised to
drive Cliff and Jean to that music festival in Indianapolis still lodged
in his gut like a permanent tumor. Coming off a night of weed and
Johnnie Walker consumption with his fellow roadies, he was too
hungover to drive, or even make the Prairie Air shuttle flight that
crashed in a storm outside of Gary later that day.

He and his young nieces were devastated, and the central
Nebraska music scene had lost the very promising Cat Scratchers.
For Dave, being a terminally single guy in dire need of redemption,
cleaning up his act, taking custody of Cliff and Jean's girls, and
finding a worthy profession seemed the least he could do. Of course,
fatherhood—or as he coined it, "extreme unclehood"—took some
getting used to, but he'd known Trish and Frannie since they were
born, and they'd always called him "Funny Uncle-Face". Years
passed, and with tears subsided and mutual trust cemented, the
arrangement had pretty much worked out. Now, with the girls deep
into high school, he wasn't sure he'd be able to afford college for both
of them (something artsy for Trish, God only knew what for Fran),
but he'd cross that canyon when he had to.

Dave pulled into their driveway, slowing even more to wave to
Meg Strump, the hard-shelled widow across the street who was
bagging leaves in the waning light with a signature Marlboro in her
mouth. The Dunwoodys had a good-sized garage around the back,
and as Dave rolled up, its double doors swung open from the inside,
and Trish and Fran scooted out. They were in the garage a lot, usually
poring through old teenage girl magazines and what not, but Dave
had a pretty long leash on them with little desire to be anything more

than a caring uncle. He frowned and put down his window.

"I hope you guys weren't smoking in there."

"Are you kidding?" asked Fran, "Cancer candy?"

"I have a new school project," piped up Trish, sliding toward the house. "Fran was helping me look for a tool."

"No kidding. What's the project?"

"Nothing. It's dumb. We gotta go finish the mashed potatoes."

They disappeared through the screen door into the kitchen. Dave mildly shook his head, pulled the Volvo into the garage. Climbed out, looked over his workbench, which didn't look touched. Sniffed the air for a second and headed into the house.

* * *

It wasn't a large kitchen—none of the rooms were—but had a nice L-shaped serving area, and the dining table fit nicely into a windowed alcove that looked out on their backyard pond, which either glimmered blue on sunny days or resembled a Scottish bog the rest of the time.

Trish and Fran always helped make dinner on weeknights, though on this occasion they seemed more focused and less chatty than Dave was used to. While he sliced up the leftover pot roast, Trish spooned out the mashed potatoes and Fran strained the peas in near silence. A tiny flat screen TV beside the sink was tuned to the E! Network, which wasn't that unusual given the girls' consuming interest in the celebrity world, though dinner preparation viewing was often his choice, and he would have preferred an old Bond movie or rock biopic.

"How was school today?"

"Not as boring," said Trish. "Ms. Koonce sprained an ankle during P.E. and we got to watch an old movie. *Footloose*."

"Oh, I remember that one. Started a dance craze for about two weeks."

"Right," said Fran. "And it had that actor Kevin Bacon who's related to everyone."

They sat down to eat. Dave instinctively grabbed the remote to kill the TV but Trish coughed loudly and nudged her sister.

"Hey Uncle Dave, can we leave that on tonight?" Fran asked.

"Why? You know we don't do that—"

"It's part of my project," said Trish quickly. "We have to make sort of a diorama thing. About our favorite entertainers. You know, movie stars, musicians."

"I know who they are. What class is this for?"

"Oh...Communication skills. Mr. Granger can get pretty out there. You can keep the volume down."

Dave sighed, mildly annoyed, and dug into his pot roast. They ate quietly, Cliff and Jean's empty place settings on one side of the table gathering dust again. It had been more than a decade since the crash, but after Dave moved in from his dumpy single apartment across town, it was decided on a teary first night there would always be a place at the table for Mom and Dad. Now Dave just had to remind himself to change out the plates and silver more often.

Trish and Fran were still being unusually mute, eyeballing the TV screen on the counter between bites. Dave asked Trish to pass the Coke Zero and it took her so long to hear him he had to ask her again.

"You okay, Trish?"

"Huh? Oh yeah. Sorry."

Fran had her fork raised in the air, chewing her pot roast in super slo-mo. She was also gazing at the TV as the news show they were watching came back from a beauty commercial.

Today's BIG story once again: Normandie Vine to do three months of rehab at Peak Experience in Eagle Creek, Colorado! Let's check in with our team coverage...

"Oh!!" Fran nearly shouted, "Did you hear about this?"

"About what?"

"Normandie Vine! Remember? She slammed into a police car last month when she was high?"

Dave turned in his seat, briefly glanced at the screen. Saw week-old footage of a miserable Normandie in sunglasses being led out of a Beverly Hills courtroom.

"Uhh...kind of missed that one."

"Pretty cool. I mean, how close to here she's gonna be," said Fran.

"I guess. I mean I know you two are big fans, but far as I'm concerned...people like that can't be far enough away."

Fran's eyes turned glacial. "What do you mean 'people like that'? She's a talented singer and actress who's had nothing but rotten luck—"

"Fran—" butted in Trish.

"No, she's right," said Dave. "To each his or her own. Personally, though? Celebrities who eat up TV news time and cover space on every magazine in Googy's checkout line are just not my kick of champagne." He kept on eating, Normandie back to being the last thing on his mind. Silence flooded the alcove again, until Fran shot Trish a jumpy glance.

"So Uncle Dave?" asked Trish.

Dave made an inquisitive sound while he chewed, without looking up.

"Did I tell you about the Astronomy Club thing we're doing tomorrow tonight?"

"The what?"

"Umm, not sure if you heard, but there's supposed to be a meteor shower around ten o'clock, and Buddy Balfo asked me if I wanted to camp out with the club up on Willow Hill to watch it. Fran wants to go too."

Dave frowned, if only briefly.

"Didn't think you guys liked that sort of thing."

"Astronomy?"

"That...and camping."

"Yeah well, first time for everything. And Buddy's kind of cute."

"No kidding." He gave her a coy smile. Trish had been thankfully slow in the boy-meeting department, but she was 17 after all, and Dave had been wondering when someone was going to jump start her heart. Hell, there must have been at least three girls who had gotten his own valves racing before he was sixteen. For a while he had thought about sitting Trish and Fran down separately and bringing up birds, bees, and whatever, but he also knew that schools, lunchroom gossip and the Internet were handling that job now. Fran was three years younger than Trish and a lot less girly, but also very wise for her age, and seemed to have recovered from a bullying incident at a friend's sleepover that briefly depressed her. If anything, she had explained a steamy thing or two to her older sister.

"Well, I suppose if you bundle up, and keep Fran here away from the Budweiser..."

"Cool. Thanks, Uncle Dave." Fran shot her another prodding glance. "Umm, also...We were gonna take Mom's car to get there. Buddy's is already full up."

"Uh-huh. Hasn't had its cover off in a month, you know."

"Oh, we know."

"Meaning you have to get gas, get the oil changed, and check the tires if you want to drive it."

"Yeah...I've done all that before."

"Maybe we'll leave a little earlier so we can take care of that," said Fran.

Dave gave them a resigned nod. The girls put their heads down and resumed eating. Dave leaned back in his chair, groping for a new thought.

"How about your homework?"

"Oh, we'll be back in plenty of time on Sunday," said Fran. "Matter of fact, I was going to take my history book along. Heard that it's kind of fun to read in a tent."

"That it is..." His mind seemed to wander. He looked out at some swaying branches in the backyard. "The first real date I ever had was an overnight camping trip."

"Huh..." said Fran, "Never knew the outdoors was your thing."

"Used to be. Way up in McKelvie National Forest, near the South Dakota border. Original plan was for three nights with Sally Tuckworth but on the first one, this massive windstorm comes up around 2 a.m. and caves in our tent while we were asleep. So I crawl out and try to prop the thing back up but it's like a damn hurricane. Plus I had a little too much peach brandy a few hours ago so said hell with this, crawled back in, cuddled up with the side of the tent on our faces and said, 'Let's just do it in the morning'. Well, Sally asked me to drive her home the next day and didn't talk to me again." He picked up his glass of Coke Zero and took a long swig. "Just the start of a successful bachelor career."

* * *

Dana McCook hated riding his bike at night. His cruiser didn't have a light in front, he never wore bright colors, and it seemed like he came close to being sideswiped by a bouncing pickup every time he went out. Of course, this might not have resulted in bodily harm; Dana was so gangly he very well could fold into a ball and roll down the street into a grass-filled gulley. Like Trish and Fran, he was a monster Normandie fan, but it wasn't so much the girl's music or acting that attracted him, but her drama. Dana just couldn't get enough of the substance abuse and courtroom reports, and made it a point to research every drug she had taken in the last ten years.

This time, Fran's voice on his cell phone after economics class was just too enticing. Whatever had called for this emergency meeting of the Normandie Vine Club on Poplar Avenue had to be big.

He rolled up the Dunwoody driveway around 10:30 p.m. Trish and Fran's uncle was usually asleep by ten, so they could have met inside the house, but he knew before he even parked his bike that this meeting had to be in the garage, or as he called it, the Normandie Vine Poplar Avenue Archives.

He heard hushed, excitable voices inside. Walked up to the double garage doors and did their secret club knock: rap...rap...rap, pause and then rap-rap. Fran swung them open in a few seconds, strange blue ink on her fingers.

"Anybody follow you?"

"Are you serious?"

"Never more so."

Dana let out an exasperated sigh, fiddled with his earring. "I'm alone, Fran."

She shut the doors after him. Dana looked around. The girls were working on about a half dozen signs, scrawled in blue Sharpie on large white pieces of poster board, and they were spread out across Dave's workbench and the hood of his Volvo. One read WE LOVE YOU NORMANDIE, another JUST SAY NO TO BLOW, and another TALK TO US!!!

"Damn," said Dana, unzipping his purple hoodie, "Someone's been—"

"Alright!" proclaimed Fran, "Let's call this meeting of the Normandie Vine Club to order! Is everyone here?"

Dana looked around sheepishly. Shrugged.

"Guess so, and if not it's their loss. Okay! We will now discuss a top secret mission, and nary a word of it will leave this garage. Understood?"

"Let's hope so," said Trish, squeaking her Sharpie on a new sign.

"Sure," said Dana, "Is this about her—"

"You've all heard by now that Normandie will be rehabbing at Peak Experience up in Eagle Creek, Colorado beginning tonight. As President and Vice-President of the club, Trish and myself will journey to said facility tomorrow morning with these signs to show her our unconditional love and support."

"Cool, except...you think she'll actually see these signs?"

"Maybe not. But she'll sure as hell hear us."

"O-kay. Only problem is I was going to start making a stew with my mom around ten, but after that I can—"

"No need, mister. Team's already assembled. Your job is to keep things under wraps here in town and at school. Not a word of this mission in any class, or at Mt. Garbage, or especially in the lunchroom."

"But that's like in three days. How long do you think—"

"We can't say. Uncle Dave thinks we're watching the meteor shower tomorrow night with the Astronomy Club. If all goes according to plan, we should return by 2600 hours on Sunday."

Dana calculated something in his head. "I think you mean 1800 hours. If you're talking 6 p.m. that is—"

"Whatever. It's still important that no one talks about this on Monday."

"You have to let me at least tell Cindy, though," said Dana, "She's the first person I listened to 'Booty Zone' with."

"Negative. She has three sisters in three different grades, and if one hears about it it's all over the school."

"Oh so what? Let them think we're cool for a few days—"

"COOL?" Fran was beside herself. "Listen, Dana. We could go there, spend a whole afternoon with Normandie downhill skiing, get drunk on malt brandy by a fireplace and show her dance routines later and no one will ever think we are cool. That car has sailed."

"They won't even take our club photo for the yearbook," added Trish despondently.

"Damn straight. They don't get Normandie's talent. They can't understand what she's going through and don't even care. I don't even think Cookie Calhoun's watched E! Channel once in her dumb life. That's why it's up to us. We're the only people who can do this. Let's make a vine for Normandie now..."

Trish laid her Sharpie on the hood, walked around the Volvo to join them. The three of them formed a circle, joined hands a little higher up on the wrist, and peered up at the dirty garage ceiling.

"We hear you Normandie..." whispered Fran.

"WE HEAR YOU!" they shouted together.

CHAPTER TWO:
EAGLE CREEK PASS

Trish carefully leaned the note against the salt and pepper shakers on the table. Sunrise was a half hour away, and she had to put on the sink light to make sure the thing was propped up facing the hallway for when Dave emerged from his room.

UNCLE DAVE—
    LEFT EARLY TO HELP ROUND UP SUPPLIES AND STAKE OUT A GOOD CAMPING SPOT FOR THE GROUP. WE HAVE OUR PHONES BUT RECEPTION MIGHT BE CRUMMY. SEE YOU TOMORROW!
                                                    —LOVE T & F

Dave kept an emergency "cash stash" in a glass cookie jar behind the toaster, and after dipping into it for a couple of extra ten-dollar bills, the girls silently went out the back door, removed the canvas cover from "Old Jeannie", their mom and dad's brown Ford Focus, shook off the dead leaves and pine needles, brought the hibernating engine to life and backed out of the driveway. Fran was staring at a second note with many items scribbled on it.
    "Please tell me Skittles are there," said Trish.
    "We're covered, T."

* * *

High up on Eagle Creek Pass, in a stunningly beautiful section of the Rockies far removed from ski supply stores, Patagonia outlets, and galleries of cheesy Western art, a radiant sunrise sliced through a deep, foggy hollow. Its orange rays licked the tops of pines, painted rows of boulders, and shot through the massive, two-story windows of Peak Experience's dining hall.
    A dozen or so communal tables were gradually being filled by a

breakfast buffet line of "Peakiteers." The guests were sleepy-eyed for the most part, garbed in matching beige sweats with Peak Experience logos over the breast: a pair of hands radiating benevolently from a snowy mountain crest. The buffet had an oatmeal bar, granola station, lavish bins of exotic fruits, range-free eggs, twenty kinds of yogurt, and a pair of short-order crepe cooks. A roaring fireplace and bearded mandolin player added to the serene environment.

Suddenly the doors to the hall swung open and Chuck and Rashid, two ex-NFL linemen, burst in. They silently split up and went to work on opposite sides of the room, eyeing guests, peering under tables, giving the buffet a quick inspection. Chuck nodded at Rashid, who whispered into his wireless headset.

"Growth Café is a go."

Seconds later, Normandie was ushered through the doors, flanked by Peak Experience director Tom Pearson and a handful of assistants all wearing beige polo shirts with the same Peak Experience logo. Pearson, a 45ish Brad Pitt wannabe, also had a white wool sweater tied over his shoulders.

Normandie had been allowed to dress differently: black designer sweats, a navy visor cap that said SAVE THE PENGUINS, and custom-made Ugg workout boots. She looked beyond exhausted, and her red hair was sticking up through her visor so that it resembled a long, knotted fuse.

"Any allergies to soy?" asked Pearson as he walked her toward the buffet.

"No."

"Tofu?"

"Uh-uh."

"Farm-raised Navaho beets?"

"Nope."

"Organic food of any kind?"

"You think I could just eat now?"

"Sure, sure. Let's get you a tray—"

"I can do it."

She started to reach for one and Chuck stepped in. Yanked a

length of grapple cord out of a dispenser on his belt, clamped one end on the buffet counter and held back a half dozen Peakiteers about to take their food. Normandie rolled her bloodshot eyes, a bit ashamed but too tired to resist the privilege. She quickly chose one of practically every item, while the servers smiled and stumbled over each other to help fill her plate.

A rich-looking kid with the jitters slipped out of line and approached her. "Hey Normandie!" She jumped as if he were a political assassin. Rashid instantly blocked the kid's path. "I played your music at my Bar Mitzvah," the kid said, "Think I could just get an auto—"

"No," blurted Rashid. "You may not."

The kid slunk away. Normandie finished collecting her food and turned into the room. Chuck's grapple cord went back into its dispenser with a loud zip. Rashid cleared a path through the area even though none was needed, and walked her to one of the few open single tables along the window. It had a spectacular mountain view. Normandie felt a bit dizzy looking at this view, and she wasn't exactly sure why.

Maybe it was because Myra Harp was already seated at the table.

"Do you need this tattooed on your scrotum, George?" she hissed into her cell phone, "No copy approval, no cover story. Thank you." She hung up, made the phone vanish inside one of her long-nailed hands and looked up at Normandie and Pearson with an icy grin.

"Good morning!"

"Will this table work for you, Normandie?" asked Pearson.

"She's fine, thanks," said Myra before Normandie could utter a syllable.

"Good, good," continued Pearson, pulling back Normandie's chair and fidgeting with her food plate to make sure it was perfectly centered between the silverware. "Let me remind you that Daybreak Ankle-Stretching begins in 45 minutes. Advanced Yoga sessions will be running all day. The Noon Tofu Delight opens at 12:30, and what else...Oh yes! The Sunset Tabla Circle—"

"Tom?" asked Myra sweetly, "Can you get lost?"

Chuck and Rashid, on either side of him, gave Pearson matching murderous stares until he finally nodded and wordlessly backed away. Normandie chewed slowly on a melon ball while Myra produced her phone again and eyed the number she had just used.

"These editors. I don't care if you smashed into the lobby of the Chinese Theater. Myra Harp's ground rules do not change. Like your suite?"

Normandie shrugged. "The usual luxurious crypt. Thanks."

Myra scrolled through her Twitter feed, ignoring the negative comment as if it were a gnat in her ear. She was 53 going on 22, sporting a blonde Normandie-inspired spike-do, blinding tangerine pants suit and far too much makeup. "Better than Malibu Gardens, that's for sure."

"Well. At least at Malibu Gardens I could play guitar once in a while."

"Right. But that place had more leaks than Kate Winslet's stateroom. You'll be fine here, Normie. Tom and I go back to Pali High, and they even have an herbal astrologist."

Normandie took a careful sip of some olive green mystery juice. "That's supposed to comfort me?" She swallowed and made a yucky face. Myra snatched a passing busboy with one of her claws.

"Can you bring her something else to drink that won't generate a lawsuit? Thank you." She looked back at her Twitter feed. "Did you take your pills? The last thing we want is another Toxic Gecko."

Normandie half-nodded. Gazed woozily at the pastoral mountaintops. A large bird with a white head was wheeling over some nearby trees and she couldn't take her eyes off it.

"Stay with me, Normie..." Myra was waiting for her to focus again, if you could call it that. "Anyway. I'll be in Aspen the next few days while you're getting settled. Got issues with anything here, find Chuck or Rashid."

"How long...do you think..."

"Don't you watch your own news? Three months. Basically ninety days of relaxing and regrouping and a hot tub or sauna whenever you want. I should only have that imprisonment."

Normandie stared at her. Her eyes were trying to well up but couldn't. Her voice quivered.

"I can't be anywhere that long. It's bullshit…"

"Honey? This country's been running on bullshit since Columbus landed in the Azores." She set her phone down. Took Normandie's wrist with her sun-shriveled hands.

"When have you ever gone wrong listening to me. Huh? Hasn't Myra always known best?"

Normandie couldn't look at her, even though she knew she was right.

"Three months at this crunchy vacation palace, that's all I ask. The minute you walk out of here, Rondo Moroni is going to sign papers on your Italian jeans deal, and we'll all be driving Maseratis by Easter, give or take—"

"I DON'T CARE!!" Normandie grabbed two melon balls, squeezed them into orange pulp and mushed them into the freshly ironed tablecloth. Guests seated at the other tables who weren't already sneaking glances at the damaged famous person in their midst spun in their chairs. Myra merely arched an eyebrow.

"Should we have a phone session with Dr. Myron today, hon? I know for a fact he isn't golfing."

"No…" Normandie uttered, sinking as low as she could possibly sink in her chair. "No Myron…"

* * *

Fran had her bare feet up on the Focus' dashboard as she slurped a giant Diet Cherry Quench-ee. They were somewhere in Eastern Colorado on Interstate 80, windswept brown plains filling three of the four horizons. Trish was in the far right lane and not exactly hot-footing it.

"It's so weird how it looks like you're getting close to the Rockies for about half a day," she mused. Far ahead, a jagged mirage of forlorn mountain peaks lined the horizon.

"Wouldn't be half a day if you went over 60 miles an hour. The speed limit on this road's only like 80, right?

"It's 75. And I'm not taking any chances, Fran. We had more than enough time this morning to check the oil and tires before leaving Endeavor."

"Yeah, right. And listen to Heck Skinner's zillion snoopy questions about where we were going? Nope."

They had made time for a supply run at Sam's Speedy Mart near the entrance to the I-80. Using bills from Dave's cash stash, they'd loaded up on fountain drinks, two family bags of Fritos, a pair of sketchy turkey sandwiches, Red Bulls for later (just in case), the new issue of *National Enquirer* with its NORMANDIE BACK IN THE TANK story taking up the bottom half of the cover, two Milky Way Midnights and a two-pound bag of Skittles—commonly known as Normandie Vine's favorite guilty treat—which they intended to toss in her general direction if they saw her.

Trish could hardly believe they were doing this. Sure, her and Fran had liked most of the same artists for years—especially ones with dynamic voices that reminded them of their mom—but Normandie was just so heartfelt and cool the first time they heard her, and becoming serious fans was as natural for them as putting on socks.

"Ha!" exclaimed Fran, snapping an inside page of the *Enquirer* as she read, 'Normandie is ready to give up men altogether because as she puts it, they're predictable, selfish dork brains.' I knew she was a lesbian!"

"Don't be stupid" said Trish. "She is not one of those. Why do you always say that?"

"I don't know...Maybe I dreamed it once."

"Well, I'd stop reading that junk. Half of it is made up."

"How do you know?"

"I just know, okay? Celebofizz is the only reliable news source on Normandie."

"Fine," said Fran, tossing the paper in the back seat. "Let's run through Operation Support again."

Trish veered the car a bit to the right to let a Peterbilt blow past them, then sighed.

"Alright...After you show her the postmortem O.D. pictures, I take her hand real gently and say, 'The only good drugs are good friends.'"

"Actually, now that I think about it...I'm the one who came up with that."

"So?"

"So maybe I should be the one who says it."

"It doesn't matter who says it, Fran."

"Yeah, but this operation was my idea."

"And I'm doing all the driving! Which I think makes it my choice."

Fran sulked briefly, fished out her cell phone. "Whatever. But if we all go to lunch I get to sit next to her." She popped her earbuds in and found a song. Trish re-fixed her gaze on the distant peaks, which just may have gotten a few feet closer.

* * *

Normandie sat alone on a long plush couch in her private A-frame suite, trying to will herself to sleep. A new age musical bastardization of Enya wafted from invisible speakers somewhere, and the tall window in front of her had the exact same soothing mountain view as the one in the dining hall. The problem was that she also held a glass of ice water and kept tilting it slightly as she nodded off, the intermittent cold splashes on her sweats leg jolting her awake.

Normally she would be keeping herself busy on Instagram, but her phone was in a sealed pouch somewhere in the complex. Probably better off, she thought. At least that twat Burton or Byron or Brynmar or whatever his name was who'd been cyber-stalking her off and on since their two-nighter during his European tour with Mashed Unit a year ago would be sending his endless sleazy texts into a black hole.

Rashid entered from a back room and cleared his throat.

"There's a motion yoga class in five minutes. How about we try for this one."

"How about we don't?"

"Well, the instructor's counting on you. Says you inspired him."

Normandie just threw her head back, stared up at the A-frame's cathedral-like ceiling.

"Oh fut the wuck…"

Rashid walked over, picked her zippered hoodie off the floor.

"Hang on a second," she said, "Just want a bite of an energy bar…"

She rose, walked to a pile of her stuff on a kitchenette counter. Carefully opened the wrapper of an energy bar that had been opened before and slid out a small plastic sheet of pills marked Klonopin. Slipped two into her mouth along with a chunk of bar and joined Rashid at the suite's door.

* * *

The Peak Experience Yoga Yard was walled in on three sides, its large flat area for mats dug out of a slope and dotted with plants and water features. A catchy Grace Jones tune from the '80s was playing when Rashid opened the entrance door from the building and Normandie staggered outside. The sun blinded her for a moment, but she could make out everyone turning to look at her—including a very skinny, bearded, and proudly flaming instructor in a lime green leotard.

"Welcome, new Peakiteer!" he announced, "Everyone? Normandie is here to let go with us!" The few participants who weren't stuck in impossible body positions applauded. Normandie grinned woozily, turned to her bodyguard.

"I got this, Rashid."

"Positive?"

"At the moment? Right now? Currently? As we speak? Definitely."

Rashid muttered something into his shoulder mic and went back in the building. Normandie gravitated to an empty mat in a back corner of the yard, beside a gurgling rock fountain and tall hedge. The instructor lowered the music, seemingly for her benefit.

"Just to get our new guest up to speed, this morning we are doing Showga, a new form of yoga that incorporates deep breathing with stylish poses. It is very popular in Europe, and what better time to introduce it to Peak Experience then on the day Normandie joins our healthy family!" He fiddled with the sound system behind him. "Sorry Grace, we'll get back to you later…"

"My Bad and You're Mad", one of Normandie's older syntho-funk hits, ruptured the cool, quiet air. A guest or two squealed with delight, one of them being the rich kid from the buffet line a few mats over. He gave Normandie a giddy thumbs-up, and she tried her best to return the smile without vomiting.

"Ready now? Everyone inhale and...STRIKE YOUR POSE!"

The group froze in assorted poses like actors in a non-existent photo shoot, most with legs bent, hands splayed out and heads thrown back, arrogant supermodel expressions all around. Normandie, who was both appalled and really starting to feel the effects of the Klonopin, chose to just stand there with hands on her hips.

"And...EXHALE!" The instructor made eye contact with Normandie, who clearly would have been happier having two molars removed. "It's all about the pose, Normandie!"

"I know, I know, I know, I know...Got this nuclear headache all of a sudden. Just give me a few, okay?"

"Let your body freeze and breathe! Let's do that again now, one and two and—"

She turned to the side this time, but with the same disinterest. Some of the group members glanced back mid-pose to see what she was doing. Normandie's powerful vocals echoed down the slope, scaring off any nearby wildlife.

You think it's a fad
When we get oh so rad
So just drop it a tad
My bad and you're mad

"And...EXHALE!"

She dropped her hands, woozily pretended to move to the song's beat. This place was a joke, she thought. Malibu Gardens was smaller and had worse food, but she could keep to herself there, even sneak in a few phone calls to friends. Here she felt like a chipmunk, caught in a valley under circling hawks.

"Breathing and preening, people! That's the key! Just go rogue and find your vogue!"

Normandie was ready to pass out. Then something rustled and cracked in the corner of her ear. She turned. A narrow section of hedge had swung open, and a gardener had entered the yard toting a hoe. He quickly shut the camouflaged gate and headed around to the far side. Normandie studied him, kept moving the best she could to the music. Whatever headache she might have had began to magically dissolve.

* * *

Eagle Creek Center was a dusty tourist trap, halfway up a twisting Rockies road that was flanked on all sides by snow-flecked peaks. The Focus was parked in the lot of a roadside general store called Gift Gulch, and Fran was bent over the hood, trying to piece together four Google maps of the area she had printed out the night before. Trish exited the store behind her, munching on something, phone glued to her eyes.

"Did you get Dana's text?"

"Think I felt it on my butt..."

"He wants an update."

"I was afraid of that."

"Should I just tell him to go to Walmart's and buy himself a life?"

"That'll work...Now was it Craggy Creek Road or Craggy Creek Trail?"

"Huh? I thought it was called Eagle Creek."

"That's the town. I'm looking for the turnoff."

"Well... Kind of hard to drive on a trail, right?"

"Good point..."

"They didn't have the directions on their site?"

"It's an exclusive secret place, Trish. We're lucky it even mentioned the state."

There was a sudden roar behind them, and a large delivery van from some place called HEALING HEALTH SUPPLY CO. screeched around a corner and up a nearby side road they hadn't noticed. Fran looked at Trish. then at the map, and saw the road was called Craggy Creek.

"Worth a try?"

* * *

The van disappeared around a bend almost immediately, but Old Jeannie chugged up after it with confidence. Fran was stoked, dug through Trish's Gift Gulch bag between their seats. "Turkey jerky! Want some?"

"Nope. Kind of watching the road right now."

Fran shrugged, tore some off for herself. "Wonder if her hair is up or down."

"I say it's up. You know, for all that stretching and stuff."

"She is just gonna FAINT when she sees our signs!"

As they climbed, yellow quaking aspens began to sprinkle the hillsides between the pines. The more steep and twisty the road became, the less the girls talked. Trish had to put the Focus into first gear at one point to maneuver a terrifying, impossible switchback at a fifty degree angle. They approached a scenic view rest area on the right. Fran got Trish's attention.

"Hey, should we stop and give the eng–"

She saw the area was just fifteen feet wide, had a wobbly guard rail and a drop on the other side of about 400 feet onto some boulders.

"Never mind."

Two more excruciating miles passed. They rounded yet another sharp bend, and finally spotted a large wooden structure through the oncoming pines.

"That's it!" yelled Fran, "They had a photo on the site!"

Trish exhaled, dried one of her sweaty hands on her pants leg. The road dropped into a small dip, then over a rise. Their faces throbbed with nervous excitement. The trees parted before them.

And Trish slammed on the brakes.

Colorado State Police had set up a roadblock just in front of the building. Cars and TV news vans clogged both sides of the narrow road, and a mob of maybe a hundred fans and reporters were clustered at the barricade.

"Shoot," said Trish.

"Shit!" said Fran.

The Healing Health supply truck had obviously been let through, because the road snaked down and around to a facility parking lot beside the giant A-frame Peak Experience structure.

"I can't believe this..." Trish continued, on the verge of tears, "What do we do?"

Fran was already reaching for her door handle. "Question the authorities, for starters. Pull over."

She grabbed the Skittles bag and climbed out, waving Trish onto some gravel behind a pickup from Idaho. At least half of the vehicles there seemed to be from out-of-state. The Normandie fans came in all sizes and ages, and most of them had brought their own signs. Trish hurried up behind Fran, trying to read every one.

"These are so much lamer than ours!"

"Okay, shush. Let me talk to this guy..."

She strolled right up to a towering state trooper who looked like he would have preferred sitting with a coffee and a maple glazed.

"Hi, officer!" beamed Fran, "What's the deal?"

"The deal is that if you don't have a press credential, you're not getting past this barrier."

The girls peered behind him. A second area had been roped off in front of the facility door just for reporters and cameramen. Fran's face erupted.

"That's not fair! Normandie hates the press! It's US she wants to see!"

"Miss, I'm going to need you to move back."

"The hell I will! You know how far we just drove?"

"Join the club. I'm not going to ask you a second time now."

"Fran, let's go—"

"NO! She needs us!!"

The trooper laid his brown state-issued gloves on Fran's arm and Trish yanked her away. "Forget it, okay? We effed up. Should've checked the Vine Line or one of the other fan sites before we left."

"OUR SIGNS ARE BIGGER, AND THEY'RE BETTER!" Fran yelled at the gawking crowd. Turned, tripped on the gravel and the Skittles bag dropped and broke open. Trish picked up as many of them as she could and hauled her sister off.

"Okay. Everything's fine. When we get home we'll sit down, write her a nice ten-page letter—"

"Another one??"

Trish didn't reply, just got her back to the Focus.

On the other side of the police barrier, Monty Matilda had been snapping photos of the crowd and apparently heard the entire exchange with the trooper. He quickly switched to a camera with a long telephoto and swiveled the lens in Trish and Fran's direction.

* * *

The Klonopins didn't mix that well with a deep forest and jagged rocks. Normandie had slipped through the hidden gate in the yoga yard maybe thirty minutes ago, but it seemed like hours. She never did much hiking as a kid, and the one time she actually took one alone was still haunting her, a kidney stone of a memory inching through her soul that she prayed would somehow dissolve on its own. The steep wooded hillsides of Eagle Pass were like the bewitched forest from *Wizard of Oz* that had kept a blanket over her eyes as a young girl, or more recently, Fangorn in *Lord of the Rings* with those freaky walking and talking trees.

Her body was moving but she may as well have been in quicksand. The sun was climbing but little of its heat or light was penetrating the pine branches. There was nothing close to a trail. Civilization was somewhere far below, but for too long a time she had been going up, and panic was beginning to stab her. The teeming, stinky streets that night she wandered away from the Osaka arena in an anti-depressant fog five years ago were also still fresh in her mind. This was nature, fresh air, horizon-to-horizon beauty, but it may as well have been hot lava.

Wait... Didn't I already pass this boulder? Is that unholy bastard waiting for me around the next bend? Pine needles poked out of her yoga leg warmers, her knees ached, her throat felt like parchment. She stepped on a pinecone with her bare feet and howled in pain, fell on her side. The high trees creaked against each other in the dry mountain breeze, seemed to mock her. She tried to sit up but the aspen leaves under her butt were slippery and she ended up on her back, questioning her small, unforgiving universe.

A car wreck I could always imagine, or a stupid overdose, but Jesus Crap not this...

* * *

Fran stared numbly at the hair-raising decline of Craggy Creek Road as Trish worked the Focus back down it, screeching the brakes irritatingly on every turn.

"You have to figure they know what they're doing in that place," said Trish, "I mean, it costs enough."

"So what? She's only been in seven other places like it, some of them costing more than the economy of a foreign country, and she's no better off."

"Well...She still has plans for the new album next year, right? As far as I'm concerned, that has a better chance of happening if she gets good help."

"That's science fiction. But whatever." The narrow scenic area was approaching on the left. "Pull over this time."

"You're not going to jump, I hope."

"No, Trish, I gotta pee!"

Trish slowed the Focus to a crawl, put on her left blinker despite no cars being in sight and pulled into the area, parking along the wooden fence posts and broken wire that passed for a guardrail. Fran got out and walked down to the far end, which had a small precarious drop to a band of shrubs. Trish carefully exited the car on the guardrail side and followed her.

"Be careful, Fran."

"Yeah, yeah." The wind was wicked there, and Fran had to hold on to the last fence post while she scaled down the tiny bluff. Trish looked away, gazed off at the handful of cars and fireplace smoke that marked Eagle Pass Center thousands of feet below.

"We could probably use a hot toddy."

"Ha. Sounds like something Dave would say..." Fran found a spot in the middle of the blowing shrubs and dropped for her pee. "Meanwhile, someone needs to explain to me what the hell a hot toddy is."

"Don't ask me. Sounds pretty nasty, though."

Fran blurted a laugh from the shrubs. Trish was happy to hear it. A gust nearly knocked her over and she had to grab herself on a section of fence wire.

"Dang!" announced Trish, "I'm going back to the car. Need help getting up?"

"Nope!"

Trish turned, got ten yards from the Focus and stopped.

Someone was behind the wheel and starting the engine.

"HEY!!" She bolted to the car. Whoever was driving was clueless, put the transmission into drive instead of reverse and nearly swerved through the fence. Trish ripped open the passenger side door and dove in.

"What the heck do you—"

And went mute, because Normandie Vine was behind the wheel. Pale, eyes wild and bloodshot, hair dirty and terrifying, a scraped bare foot feeling for a pedal—but definitely Normandie.

"No. Way..."

"I HAVE TO GET OUT OF HERE!!"

She shoved the car into reverse and hit the gas pedal, backed into another section of fence. The rear wheel was two inches from going over the edge. Fran had run up to the car now, staring in at Normandie, unsure whether to squeal with delight, faint, or freak.

"Get her out!" Trish's voice snapped Fran awake. She rolled over the hood of the car, ripped open the driver door and quickly shoved a foot inside, smashing the brake. Normandie's forehead hit the top of the steering wheel and she fell sideways, into Trish's arms. Fran killed the engine, yanked out the keys, helped pull a dazed Normandie out of the front seat.

"It's really her, right?" asked Trish. "We're not having one of those shared hallucinations?"

"Hallucinations don't try and steal your car—"

"NO MORE POSING!!!" Normandie's voice echoed weirdly down the rock wall canyon. The girls quickly dumped her into the back seat, slammed the door.

"She's right!" said Fran, "Get us out of here!"

"Okay, but—"

"But nothing!"

"Yeah, but...down or up?"

"What do you think??" Fran hopped back in the passenger seat. Trish hesitated a moment, then heard far-off police sirens and saw two fresh state trooper cars screeching up the mountain road, maybe three curves away.

"Let's go, damn it!" yelled Fran from inside the Focus. Trish got in, started the engine. In the back seat, Normandie's eyes were half-lidded, her muddled blatherings lowered to a whisper.

"No Myron today..."

"Who the hell's Myron?" asked Fran.

"She's on something," said Trish, steering the Focus back down the road.

"Wouldn't you be, stuck in that place?"

"Need Chapstick..."

Fran turned, saw that Normandie's lips were cracked and bleeding at the corners. She unscrewed a bottled water and tried to hand it to her. Normandie gaped at the bottle like it was an alien probe, so Fran splashed a little on her mouth.

"Here they come!" said Trish. The trooper cars were just a hundred yards away. Fran gave Normandie's shoulder a nudge, and she thankfully fell on her side, below windshield level. The girls held their breath, froze and stared straight ahead until the troopers blew past them.

"Okay," said Fran, patting her sister's leg, "Stay careful, but a little faster."

"Faster? Are you nuts? This road is the front seat of a roller coaster, Fran. And we don't need to get her sick."

Fran looked at Normandie again. She was sprawled on the seat, officially passed out, the water on her lips replaced with a smidgen of drool.

"Is she dead?"

"Nope. Breathing. Permission to speed up a little."

Trish gritted her teeth, bumped the car up to 30 miles an hour. "I almost can't believe what I can't believe anymore," she said. "This is insane!"

"Hey, Normandie escaped from Healthy State Penitentiary, and somehow ended up in our car. As far as I can tell, that's a miracle."

"Of course it is! Except…"

"Yeah?"

Trish glanced at their stowaway in the rear view mirror, whispered when she didn't really have to. "Except what are we doing with her?"

Fran coolly took out her cell phone. "Okay, it's a little after four. If we book it, we can make it back to Endeavor by midnight."

Trish nearly drove off the cliff. "You're not serious."

"What did you think we were doing?"

"Not that!"

"What then? Drop her off at the nearest hospital or TV station so they can stick her back in the hell machine and hit spin?"

"She's a famous person, Fran. Everybody and their mother will be looking for her—"

"Right. And we got her. Who better to take care of Normandie than her most loving fans? Nobody even has to know."

"How can they not? What the heck is Uncle Dave going to say?"

Fran grinned slightly. "I'll deal with Dave. You drive."

CHAPTER THREE:
DAMAGE CONTROL

Elm Road Cemetery was quieter than usual, because for once, the wind wasn't blowing. It seemed like every time Dave visited Cliff and Jean's graves, he spent more time clearing grass, dead leaves, and tumbleweeds away from the headstones than he did leaving flowers. No doubt about it, Dave noticed the second he climbed out of the Volvo with a plastic shopping bag and his mini-boom box: The air was thick and still, with some odd, waffle-shaped clouds coagulating on the horizon. *Maybe they'll even be able to hear the new song...*

He walked by the oldest grave markers, the plain wooden crosses and little cracked stones from the 1800s, many with the same last names. Delbert Boggs had actually been cremated, and now there was just a plaque affixed to a boulder for him in Endeavor Square calling him FATHER OF OUR TOWN that birds occasionally squirted on. Many townspeople thought old Delbert would've been happier in the prairie grass out here at the end of Elm Road, but maybe that was the price of too much fame.

Cliff and Jean's plots were just past the fourth elm. They were made of simple white marble, both with the same D. 8/30/05 chiseled into them, and a plaque set into the grass reading

YOU'RE RUNNING WITH ME
DON'T TOUCH THE GROUND
WE'RE RESTLESS HEARTS
NOT THE CHAINED AND BOUND

Bryan Ferry was one of his older brother's more modern favorites, and using lyrics from the rhapsodic "Slave to Love" seemed appropriate.

"Hi guys," Dave began as always, pulling out his little picnic blanket, along with a Saran-wrapped cold cut sandwich and small bag of Sun Chips. He set the boom box on the ground a few feet in front of the headstones and switched on the CD function. Dave, a notorious technology holdout his entire life, may have been the last person in Nebraska to get an ATM card. He also bought one of the last portable cassette/CD players a few years back, and was so fearful of any "futuristic" replacement that he had gone right back the next day and bought a second one he had yet to open.

"Check out this newer version of 'Oakie Boogie' that I found at the Music Bucket. Gal's name is Ella Mae Morse and it really swings." He pushed play, and bounced one of his Dockered legs to the rhythm while he bit into his sandwich. Jean, who loved old country music, and Cliff, who managed her and could play and belt out their killer electric cover of "Walkin' After Midnight" in their shows, never met a Patsy Cline song he didn't like.

"Sweet, huh? All I knew was the Jack Guthrie version, but this one's from '51. And guess who that is on pedal steel? Speedy West!" The headstones had no reaction, but Dave smiled warmly regardless.

"Girls are off on an overnight with the Astronomy Club. In the Focus, just so you know..." He dug out a can of Coke Zero and popped it open. "Haven't heard from them since they peeled off the cover this morning, so I guess it's driving just fine." He washed the sandwich down with the soda. "Not sure what we're all doing for Thanksgiving yet. The Goshens invited us over again, but Trish says she has a new stuffing recipe with nutmeg, so we'll see how that goes...Oh—and Fran's got an A in history again, pretty great. Not sure she'll ever pull one of those off in math, but at least she's trying."

The song ended, and a gust of wind came out of nowhere. Dave quickly grabbed the food wrapping. "Must have been windy a lot around here, huh? Got no clue where those white roses blew." He reached back in his plastic bag, lifted out the final item, a small cactus plant. "Anyway, this one should stick around, if you know what I mean." He dug out a small hole in front of the headstones for it with a spoon, secured the thing in the ground. "Just don't you two be leaning over to smell it at night."

Satisfied with his garden work, he stood up and looked around the cemetery. A feral grey dog that could just as well have been a coyote was trotting along a nearby road. Off to the west, the waffle-shaped clouds had darkened, become long pancake layers.

"Damn. Don't like the looks of that. Hang on a second, guys." He fumbled in his jacket pocket, took out his cell phone. It was the cheapest and oldest Nokia that still worked that he could possibly have. He flipped it open and shielded his eyes to be able to find Trish's speed dial number. Walked a yard or two away from the gravesite while it rang.

"Hello!" said her message, "It's Trish Dunwoody! What's going on?" The beep took forever to beep.

"Uh hey Trish, it's Uncle Dave. I just wanted to...Before you settle on a campsite and everything, it may be a good idea to check the weather forecast. You can do that on your phone, right? Not sure how warm you guys are dressed...and stuff. Call me back, okay?" He closed the phone and returned to the graves. Cliff and Jean hadn't gone anywhere.

"I'll probably just send her one of those text messages later." He folded up the picnic blanket, made sure he had all his trash, then laid a gentle hand on each headstone. "Okay, love birds. See you again soon." He exhaled and walked away.

* * *

At the Aspen Fur Barn, Maya Harp stood in front of a mirror, trying on a succession of fur hats with the help of a rugged but dashing salesman. She was also on her cell phone's earbud mic and looked anything but relaxed.

"That's not what I asked. What I asked was how much am I paying you two mesomorphs?" Her eyes exploded. "ME-SO-MORPH. It's a scientific term, Chuck, meaning overpaid ex-steroid junkie who can't find a birthmark if it's on his own ass!" The salesman plopped a new Russian shearling hat on her head that nearly swallowed it whole. Myra shook her hair violently until the thing tumbled off.

"Yes, you already told me that. The landscape man. Are you serious?? One underpaid Latino leaves a gate unlocked and the most valuable entertainment commodity in America disappears like Tinker Bell? People are going to bleed for this, Chuck, and Hector Gonzalez Martinez Jr. will not be one of them. Who's the police idiot I need to talk to?"

The salesman held out a black sheepskin "Elmer Fudd" hat. Myra knocked it out of his hand. Then her phone vibrated.

"Text me his name. I have another call." She thumbed a button. "Myra here."

In a sleek, palm-adorned, high-rise office in Century City, a bald British press agent filed his nails next to a speakerphone.

"Sorry to hear the news, my dear."

"Top o' the goddamn morning, Simon. And I have no quotes for you."

"I wouldn't be so hasty to be bitchy, Myra. Not when I hear at least five editors worldwide are contemplating Normandie cover stories."

In Colorado, Myra's cell phone suddenly got sweaty in her hand. "Do tell."

"I just did. The world is in complete turmoil, yet all anyone wants to read about is the disappearance of Normandie Vine. Funny how that works for us."

Myra screwed up her face. If there was one thing she learned, it was to never give up your power. "I'd say a few more covers might change my mind. Like...a dozen?"

Simon smiled. "I'd wager that's a possibility, dear. So...any leads on her yet?"

"Not even a taste. But...there's a slight possibility I'll be in touch with you after the first crumb."

* * *

What little daylight still existed on Interstate 80 was nearly gone. Trish put on Old Jeannie's right clicker and Fran, who had been dozing beside her, snapped awake. Saw them exiting the highway.

"Why we getting off?"

"Because we need some gas. Unless you want to help push us back to Nebraska."

They rolled into a dusty lot for Lulu's Place, a combination café, convenience store, and gas station. Beyond, fifty miles of nowhere lay in every direction. Fran peered into the back seat at Normandie, curled up like a homeless tabby and snoring in little steam valve bursts.

"She's still out," said Fran.

"I know. It makes me wonder what she was on."

"Could've been her Xanax again. But that's not usually this strong. Unless she took two of them."

"Or three..." Trish pulled up to the most isolated pump she could find and killed the engine. She looked concerned again.

"Should we look through her pockets?"

"Naw. Let her sleep. I'll get us a couple more Red Bulls while you gas up."

"Okay, but hurry! And don't be weird while you're in—"

"It's cool, Trish. I got this." She winked and climbed out. Trish waited a few moments, glanced in her rear and side windows, then got out and unscrewed the gas cap. Fran seemed to be taking her sweet time walking into the store. Trish grumbled to herself, began to gas up the car and felt something throb in her coat pocket. She took out her cell phone and saw MESSAGE FROM...DAVE lit up. She groaned, began to listen to it but Normandie's foot suddenly thumped on the back seat door.

"Don't WANNA!" she cried in her sleep. Trish re-pocketed the phone, looked through the glass. Normandie was still comatose, but had rolled over. A swath of red hair was stuck to the roof of her mouth and fluttering up with every new burst from the steam valve. Trish carefully opened the back door and leaned in.

"Don't wanna leave Paula..."

Trish frowned in puzzlement. Watched her sleep while the gas pump ran on automatic behind her. She found a spot for her knee on the seat and leaned over. Plucked a few strands of Normandie's hair off her mouth like a brain surgeon, then took a finger and oh so gently wiped a bit of sweat from her cheek. The droplet stayed on

Trish's finger and she brought it close to her eyes for inspection, as if it were ash from Vesuvius.

In the convenience store, Fran paid for the Red Bulls and a new giant bag of Skittles. Looked up at a muted TV that had a live report on the SEARCH FOR NORMANDIE VINE. Helicopter views of cops with dogs in hilly woods. Fran turned pale, got her change and hurried back out.

The gas pump clunked, capping off. Trish withdrew from the back seat and saw a flustered Fran already standing there.

"I thought you wanted her to sleep," said Fran, looking unusually out of sorts.

"I did. I mean I do." Trish softly shut the back door and replaced the gas nozzle. "Does she know anyone named Paula?"

"Not that I know of. Why?"

"I thought I heard her say that name." Trish got back in the car, started the engine. "Maybe we should uh, leave some Skittles on the back seat, just in case she wakes up."

"Better if she doesn't," said Fran, slightly rushed. "Let's book."

"Did something happen in there?"

She shook her head, popped open a Red Bull and guzzled down half of it. "Let's just say Normandie isn't just all over the news…She IS the news."

* * *

Dave sat alone at the dinner table, chewing a final hunk of leftover pot roast. Hitchcock's *Notorious* was on the kitchen TV, but as Cary Grant tended to a sick, poisoned Ingrid Bergman in bed, Dave picked up the remote and started surfing channels. Game show. Golf channel. Latino soap opera. Some CNN live report with helicopter views. He gobbled a few peas and flipped to the Weather Channel. The western portion of Nebraska had a red circular blemish on it the size of a pizza. Dave grimaced, rose, and grabbed his cell phone off the counter. He dialed Trish's number.

"Hey again, it's your uncle. Where are you guys? The weather's getting a lot worse so I hope you're safe. Please call, okay?"

He hung up, put the phone on the counter. Looked at the TV screen. Grabbed the phone again and sat down at the table with it. Pushed his plate aside to be able to concentrate.

After stabbing a few wrong buttons on the Nokia, he found the one for messaging. A cursor blinked. He began typing, one tentative finger at a time:

HI TRISH. MESSAGING YOU NOW. THERE'S A STORM WHERE U ARE CAMPING I THINK. I AM NOT LOL-ING. CALL PLEASE.

He knew this wasn't a Western Union telegram, but couldn't help writing it like one. After finishing, his finger hovered in the air over the little screen, before it hit an EXIT button and wiped out the entire message. He growled a barely audible obscenity, then began to type the thing all over again.

* * *

It was like driving into a cotton ball. The eastern sky was dark, but little frozen white pellets flew horizontally out of the gloom and straight into the windshield. Neither Trish nor Fran had spoken a word for at least half an hour. The Focus crawled along ethereal interstate 80, following one lane of semi-visible tire tracks and a pair of ghostly red taillights that were probably just thirty yards in front of them but looked more like one hundred.

"Do you think we're close to Kearney yet?" asked Trish.

"See a sign?"

"I can't read any signs. Check your map thingamajig."

Fran took out her phone but it was making a little sorry face. "Crap. Out of juice."

"Use mine then. It's in my right pocket." Fran reached over, fished into her sister's coat. Took out Trish's magenta-covered iPhone and saw Dave's text glowing at her.

"Whoa. Uncle Dave texted us."

"That's impossible."

"He's worried about the weather. Thanks for that. Looks like he also called. Twice."

"Should we call him back?"

"Yeah, maybe later. After we figure out what the hell to tell him."

"Well, you're better at lying than I am."

"Hey! My lies always come from a good place."

"Unless we just...tell him the truth."

"What, that we have Normandie Vine in the back seat of our car? I'm sure that'll go over big."

"He's going to find out sooner than later, right?"

"Right. I vote later. And—LOOK OUT!"

The red lights in front of them suddenly blossomed. Trish slammed the brake and the Focus skidded into a 180 turn. She lurched the wheel in the opposite direction as she'd been taught, but a ditch in the highway median got to them first. The back tires fell in, vaulting the front of the car up like a torpedoed cargo ship. The girls screeched and Fran tumbled into the back seat, landing right on top of Normandie.

"HEY!!" Normandie cried, shaking to life. She threw a wild hand out, grabbed Fran by the collar of her jacket. "What's your—problem..." Her eyelids fluttered, and her grip on Fran's collar relaxed. She was still only half-conscious.

"Ssssh..." said Fran, instinctively, "Everything's fine. Go back to sleep..." She carefully removed Normandie's hand from her collar, laid it back down on the seat.

"Are you okay?" whispered Trish.

"Yeah. You?"

"Think I might have a bloody lip—"

"SHIT."

"What's wrong?" Fran did a few contortions to climb off Normandie, was groping around on the car's tilted floor.

"Bunch of stuff fell out of her sweats..."

"Anything interesting?"

"Naw...Hair clips...Some kind of snack bar, I think." She saw the sheet of Klonopins protruding out the top of the bar, and slid them completely out.

"Jeezus to Betsy…"

"What are those?"

"Something super-ass strong, you can bet on that."

The quick whoop of a police siren made them jump. Normandie stirred again, attempted to re-open her eyes. A state trooper vehicle was approaching, filling the scene with blue bubble light. It stopped a few capsized cars away and a trooper sporting a fur hat with earflaps climbed out, armed with a flashlight. Began checking on every car.

"Yikes!" blurted Trish, "What do we do?"

"Not freak out, for starters."

"He'll see Normandie!"

"Yeah. That could be an issue." Fran looked at the sheet of Klonopins in her hand, then at Normandie.

"Let's give her another one."

"What??"

"We have to. Otherwise she might give herself away. Plus we could be stuck here for hours, and then what if she wakes up? Where's the water bottle—"

Trish reluctantly handed it to her. Normandie was still on her back, the car still at its tilted angle. Fran carefully inserted another pill just inside her mouth and poured a bit of water in. Normandie choked in her sleep for a second, but the pill went down. Fran quickly peeled off the down jacket she was wearing, tossed it on top of Normandie and climbed back into the front seat as the trooper knocked on Trish's window with his flashlight. Trish opened the door and hung out of it a little to talk to him.

"You girls okay?" asked the trooper.

"Oh yeah. Just need a little help straightening out here." The trooper nodded, trying to keep his eyes on the other cars slowing to nearby stops and skids. He raised his flashlight, but from the odd angle it was hard for him to see inside the car. Instead, he reached down for a handful of snow and held it out for Trish.

"Put that on your lip. Tow man should be over soon."

"Thanks...Was there an accident up ahead?"

"Six car pileup. Road's like the Ice Capades. How far you headed?"

"Pretty far," piped in Fran. "Hoping to make it to St. Louis tomorrow."

"Well, hang tight. Hopefully we'll have you on your way in less than an hour."

He started back to his cruiser. Trish shot Fran a frozen stare.

"St. Louis??"

"No sense telling him about Endeavor, Nebraska, right?"

Trish stared off into the blowing snow. It was tough to tell what direction she was even looking in. "Shoot. Another hour. We better text Dad back."

"Okay, and say what?"

"I don't know, Fran. Make something else up."

* * *

Dave stood at the bathroom mirror, methodically flossing his teeth. Patsy Cline sang "I Fall to Pieces" from his bedroom, but he was too anxious to hum along. His cell phone chirped suddenly, and he fished for it in his terrycloth bathrobe pockets for a good ten seconds. Hurriedly flipped it open and located the new text:

HI UNCLE DAVE, WEATHER AT CAMPSITE GOT BAD. WE'RE HANGING AT SOME FRIENDS OF STEVE RICKLEY'S IN ARNOLD AND PLAYING TOMB RAIDER AND WITCHER 3. SHOULD BE HOME IN FEW HOURS AND NO DRINKING OR DRUGS SO DON'T WORRY AND GOOD NIGHT!

Dave took a relieved breath and resumed his flossing.

* * *

It was closer to two hours before the Focus began to move again. Things got a little intense when the tow truck guy righted the car, but except for a strange moment when Normandie whispered "Want Santa...", she stayed happily comatose throughout. The blizzard turned into snow showers, then a drizzle by the time they reached the Nebraska state line.

Normandie remained asleep and immobile even after they exited the interstate and hit the two-lane roads, the girls holding their breath with every bump Trish drove over or pothole she swerved around.

"So where we gonna put her?" asked Fran.

"Where do you think? My mattress is way more comfortable. I can just lay out my bag on the floor."

"Yeah, but you got those Normandie posters all over your damn walls. They might flip her out."

"No they won't, silly. It shows that we love her."

"That isn't love, Trish. It's worship. Love was us driving across Siberia today to bring her to Nebraska."

"Yeah, well there isn't just one way to be a fan, you know."

"Whatever. What I do know is we gotta make this a four-step operation and the first step is take it slow."

"What are the other steps?"

Fran shrugged. "Tell you when I think of 'em."

* * *

It was two in the morning when they turned onto Poplar Avenue.

Across the street, Meg Strump had dozed off in a living room rocker with her Schnauzer and half-empty pint of whiskey in her lap. The gravelly sound of the Focus' tires pulling into the Dunwoody drive snapped her eyelids up. She peered through her living room blinds and saw Trish hurry up to the kitchen door of the house and swing it open.

By the time she returned to the car, Fran was half inside the back seat, leaning nervously over a still-limp Normandie.

"Oh God," uttered Trish, "We killed her."

"Nope. Breathing. Take her legs."

Trish gingerly took hold of her thin ankles. Fran wedged herself in as far as she could, secured her hands under Normandie's armpits and slid her out. Together, they carried her up to the kitchen door and ducked inside.

Across the street, Meg Trump leaned back in her rocker, frowned, and took another swig of whiskey.

* * *

As they crept down the hall, Trish peeked into Dave's room and saw him asleep on top of the bedspread, still in his robe with the Nokia phone balanced on his belly.

Minutes later, Fran stood a few feet from her bed, hypnotically gazing at Normandie Vine asleep in it. She was tucked nicely under the egg-colored sheets and cloud print comforter, sawing redwood trees. The bed was a twin, plenty big enough for Fran to slip under there beside her, at least for a few hours, but the very idea both tingled and paralyzed her. It was as if every minute she had spent watching Normandie on television and in the movies, every magazine photo she had clipped out for her scrapbook, every abusive jab she had endured from kids at school who thought Normandie was a druggie loser, basically every shred of fandom she had mustered for her favorite famous person on earth had converged rhapsodically in this very moment, and she'd be damned if she wasn't going to stand there and slowly take it in.

Sure, Trish loved Normandie too, but that was a more blatant, embarrassing kind. The way an African bird clings to a water buffalo, or an intern in Washington follows around a Congressman. Fran was sublime, maybe even stealth; a friend who had visited L.A. and reported a few star sightings once told her that celebrities don't mind being recognized or greeted by strangers in public—they were in the business in the first place because they desired fame—but the barriers between celebrity and non-celebrity needed to be respected.

Fran was going to be a lithe panther in this strange new jungle; she would make Normandie feel at ease as many ways as possible, maybe even be the sister she knew Normandie never had.

Still: crawl into this bed with her? That was a bit much for the first night. She peered down at her sleeping bag, unused on their non-existent Astronomy Club trip, and already rolled out on the floor beside the bed. She peeled off her jeans and climbed inside, working the bag backwards with her butt so that she could lean her pillow against the wall. Not ready to jeopardize her good fortune and certainly not ready to sleep, she sat there and studied Normandie's motionless form.

After a few moments an idea came to her and she felt around on the floor for her phone, raised it in the air and snapped a flash photo of her new roommate. She admired the result, then set the phone down and attempted to shut her eyes. God only knew what would happen in the morning, but for now, Fran was exactly where she wanted to be, and was in possession of a photo she vowed to never show anyone.

CHAPTER FOUR:
THE SLEEPOVER GUEST

With his perfect cup of Beansmith's Nightingale Dark Roast brewed and poured into his black and yellow Cat Scratchers mug, Dave was ready to commence the pancakes and bacon. He had secrets for perfecting each that had been handed down in the Dunwoody family, and because he wasn't due at the clinic until around eleven, had plenty of time to "make them croon" as Grandma Roseanne always said.

Trish and Fran apparently sleeping in after their late night arrival helped as well. The snow that had attacked Colorado blew through Endeavor around three in the morning—Dave knew because the icy wind rattled his window pane and he had glanced at the clock—but otherwise, knowing the girls were home safe and not freezing somewhere in a tent had put him right back to sleep.

He got the bacon going first, natural stuff prepared out at Ed Mahoney's farm and sold at Googy's, being sure to spread the slices out evenly in a big pan and then covering them with just enough water to keep the moisture in. Fran liked hers a little more crispy so he would be sure to let a few pieces linger.

As for the pancake batter, it was stirred and sitting for its required five minutes. While the bacon began to sizzle, he took a robust swig of coffee and gazed out at the backyard pond again. Snow coated the dead leaves that filled much of it, and he reminded himself to clean them out one of these weekends when the weather didn't intervene.

A door opened in the hall, and he thought he heard Trish's voice whispering. That was different. Fran was almost always the first one up, and what in hell was there to whisper about?

"Breakfast in five, Trish!" he called.

She didn't respond.

"Trish?"

"Yeah, coming—"

Except then she didn't, disappeared into the bathroom instead and shut the door. Dave sighed, tossed a little water on the iron skillet. The droplets sizzled and danced around, but didn't evaporate. Ready.

Another door opened and closed. Fran was whispering now. Dave moved away from the stove and peered down the hall. Fran stood at the closed bathroom door.

"Frannie? Breakfast happening!"

She waved Dave an "O.K." but continued to stand there. Dave turned back to the skillet and poured four perfect batter circles into it. He adjusted the flame under the bacon. Turned back around as Trish and Fran hurried into the room and dropped silently in their chairs. Trish had her pajamas, robe and slippers on but Fran was still in her clothes and wool socks from last night. They looked like a pair of cats who had eaten separate canaries.

"Everything okay?" asked Dave.

"Sure!" blurted Fran. "We got any juice?"

"Of course...Help yourselves."

She hesitated. Trish gave her an odd stare and Fran jumped up, nearly knocking her chair over. Grabbed two glasses from the cabinet and opened the fridge.

"Smells good, Uncle Dave!" said Trish, "Great, actually..."

"See any accidents out there last night?"

Fran poured them both cranberry juice, returned to the table. Realized she had left the fridge open and jumped back up to close it.

"Yeah a pretty bad one." Trish looked at her sister again. "Right?"

"Yep. About a 46-car pileup. Trish did a great job skidding out of the way but it took forever to clear the road. Which is why we were late. Y'know. All the tow trucks and stuff."

"Wow, 46 cars? Didn't hear about that on the morning news." He plucked out the bacon, laid the strips on a set of paper towels. "What route was it on?"

"Ohh, the I-80. We got on it for a few exits on the way to our friend's."

"Fran is exaggerating a little," said Trish, "It was more like...

36 cars."

Dave turned slightly with an amused glance. Scooped the finished pancakes onto a plate and put it on the table.

"And here's ten of these flappers. Butter away!"

Fran hesitated a bit too long so Trish snatched the knife from her.

* * *

Normandie's nose moved, sniffed slightly before her eyelids even quivered. Something wonderful from the past was in the air. *A sunny Sunday morning in Chatsworth, "Heart of Gold" by that Neil Young guy playing ceaselessly on Dad's turntable while his signature bacon crackled on the stove. Mom all cheery-eyed at the table with a Virginia Slim, still a few hours away from her first vodka and tonic...*

Fran's bed creaked. Normandie rolled over, mashing her face against a Shrek squeaky doll. Her eyes snapped open like bloodshot window shades. Where the hell was she? The wall colors around her were a muted beige with army green trim. She could have sworn her room had a teal and brown thing going with Kurt Cobain posters the last time she looked.

At least Dad had that yummy bacon going in the pan—or someone did. She sluggishly sat up and rubbed her eyes. The window was a few feet away. And hold on a second. Were those naked, swaying branches through the curtain? Almost painfully, she rose to her feet and shuffled over. Squinted outside at the snow-covered grass in the side yard, the Victorian-style house next door, and her entire face softened, a delirious grin formed on her still-chapped lips and everything murky began to clear and downright glow. The sun was hurting her eyes a bit, though, so she grabbed a wacky pair of dark purple sunglasses off a dresser.

* * *

Napkin tucked into the top of his shirt, too ravenous to even enjoy his coffee, Dave gobbled his pancakes and bacon while the girls mutely pecked at theirs. It didn't escape his attention. He laid his fork down and idly massaged an old scar on one of his thumbs.

"Okay. I don't know what happened with which boy or boys last night, or what kind of inebriation was involved, but actually, you two have been a little off since I got home from work the other day." The girls said nothing. "Anyway, I don't think I'm being crazy here, so uhh...if anyone wants to 'fess up, I'm all ears and smiles."

Fran looked at Trish, who glared at Fran, who finally sighed, lowered her head and addressed the tablecloth.

"Well...Remember how you told us once that Mom and Dad said it was important to always have a goal in mind? Y'know, in our lives? Anyway, we kind of have one now—for the time being, I mean. This goal kind of dropped in our laps yesterday."

"Oh. I get it. So it has something to do with camping, or astronomy? Or driving in snow to party at a friend's house?"

"Not exactly—"

"What she means," interrupted Trish, "is that one thing led to another on this little car ride, and we um...we sort of...you know—"

"We made a new friend!" proclaimed Fran, and with that the door to her bedroom swung open and Normandie stumbled into the hall. She bounced off a doorjamb but kept moving. Her hair was in another dimension, her filthy sweats something stripped off a buried death squad victim, but then she slid a few feet into the kitchen and beheld the laid-out breakfast table. Even inside Fran's dark purple sunglasses, her face lit up like a Fourth of July sparkler.

"Good day, sunshines!" she chirped, "Where's that bacon at?"

Dave was actually sitting there holding the plate of it. He stared at Normandie with a completely baffled expression. "Aha!" she said, gliding over, "May I?" She snatched two pieces off the plate and started munching them.

Trish and Fran were equally speechless. "Excuse me," uttered Dave, peering at her, "Have we met—"

"Doubt it," said Normandie, dropping into Jean's empty chair at the far end of the table. "I mean, I know I've been going on a lot of sleepovers lately, but sure don't remember coming up here to the Grapevine."

"The Grape-what?" asked Trish.

"Anyway, has my dad called yet?"

Fran was puzzled. "Your dad??" She glanced at Trish, who was equally confused. Both of them knew that Normandie's father moved out when she was eight, right before her mom died in a freak car accident, and that she was literally raised by nannies. Most people thought it explained her recent self-destructive behavior.

Unaware of any of this, Dave slid a few pancakes onto his plate. "Does your friend have a name—"

"Amanda!!" cried Normandie, and stuck out a friendly hand. Dave reluctantly shook it but Trish and Fran were mute, and Fran was nearly pale. Words quivered in her mouth.

"Amanda...Mushnik?"

"Like duh."

Fran stood up, froze a second, then pulled Trish out of her chair and escorted her down the hall.

"Where you guys going?" asked Dave.

"Quick meeting," said Fran. Their uncle gave Normandie a bewildered look, and accidentally began buttering his bacon instead of his pancakes.

"It's impossible," whispered Fran.

"Maybe it's her cover," whispered Trish.

"She's never used a cover."

"Well, look where she just was. Maybe they brainwashed her or something."

"Trish, didn't you hear her? She thinks she's on a sleepover! In Grapetown or wherever she said. She thinks she's 12 again—"

"Oh come on."

"Come on nothing! Look how she's acting!" They peeked. Normandie was sprinkling salt on her fingers and licking them, much to Dave's dismay.

"So what are you saying? That she has amnesia? She was asleep when the car went off the road, Fran. She didn't even hit her head—"

"Wait," said Fran. She snapped a finger. "The Klonopin. We gave her one too many! I think I read that strong psychoactive drugs like that *can* cause amnesia."

"Uncle Dave might know."

"Yeah, well the hell with asking him."

"Ask Dana then. Or Google it."

"Crap. My phone's in the other room—"

"Girls?" said Dave from the table. "Aren't you're being a little rude here?" Normandie had put the salt shaker down, finished the leftover bacon from its plate and was now eyeing Trish and Fran's plates. Dave got the hint and grabbed another plate, slid a few pancakes onto it for their guest. The girls returned to their seats, totally out of sorts.

"Umm listen...Amanda," said Trish, "Was your dad supposed to pick you up?"

"You mean Juanita? Who the flam knows?"

"Who's Juanita—"

"Well, if he does it might be a good thing," said Dave, "Trish and Fran do have some homework to get done today."

Normandie stared into space and shrugged. "Yeah. That's why I asked if someone called. Hey, bet we even have time to go hang at a mall. There's one around here, right?"

"No," said Trish, "I mean, I don't think so."

Dave was now even more confused. "What mall—"

"OH. MY. GOPP!" exclaimed Normandie with a mouthful of pancake. "These are beyond righteous! Are you guys the Waltons or what?"

"The who?" asked Fran.

"Anyway..." said Dave, getting up. "Afraid I have to go to work today. No doubt there are some ailing pets that need me."

"No doubt, Dave," a jittery Trish piped up, "Just go ahead. We'll clean up!"

Dave thought he was hearing things, and Normandie kept wolfing down her pancakes. "So who's gonna drive us to the mall?" she asked.

"Actually, it's not open," said Fran. "They had some kind of big gas leak and they're fixing it."

Dave, still mystified, glanced around for his down jacket a good ten seconds, then saw it was on the back of the chair he had been sitting in. "Maybe I'll grab some takeout for tonight."

"That'll work!" said Trish. They waited silently for him to collect his leather briefcase and car keys and pull on his snow boots. The second he went out the back door their bodies visibly deflated with relief.

"So who cares about a stupid gas leak?" said Normandie.

"Look," said Trish, "Malls are kind of boring. How about we just stick around here and y'know, play music, watch TV—

"Maybe not TV," said Fran quickly.

"Right, not that."

Normandie licked her entire plate clean and belched loudly. "Now I gotta whiz."

"First door on the left," said Trish. They watched her sashay down the hall. The moment the bathroom door closed, Trish and Fran looked at each other with excited, pinwheel eyes and tried not to squeal.

"Amanda Mushnik in our house??" said Trish under her breath. "I cannot believe how incredible this is!"

"I know, right? Nobody has ever hung out with this version of her."

"At least since the 1990s—"

They cracked up, and had to jab each other's arms to keep their exuberance down.

"What should we do with her?" asked Fran after they caught their breath.

"Shoot. I don't know. But that was a good call on the no-TV thing. If her head's in the 1990s she probably has no clue about computers and smart phones."

"Oh crap. We have to hide her DVDs."

In perfect alarmed sync, they darted into the den and frantically rifled two entire shelves of a bookcase. Filled their arms with every concert, TV show and movie DVD they had of Normandie and dropped them in a wooden crate beside the couch under some wool blankets. Satisfied, Fran took out her cell phone and hurried to the coat rack by the back door.

"What are you doing??"

"Texting Dana, meeting him at Googy's as soon as they open."

"What?? Why?"

"Because he was part of Operation Support, that's why. And deserves to know what happened in Colorado."

"Are you sure? Won't Dana tell everyone in school?"

"Not if we threaten to kick his scrawny butt."

"Well, what am I supposed to do with Normandie—I mean Amanda??"

"Come on, Trish. You're older than me. You can think of things, too."

Normandie exited the bathroom, came back in the kitchen patting her gut. "Damn. I am a P-I-G pig! Can't remember the last time I ate so much." She gazed at the girls, still with half-lidded eyes. "Which one of you was who again?"

"I'm Trish, she's Fran."

"Yah. And what about the cute older dude?"

"That's Dave," said Fran, seizing the moment. "Our dad." Trish gave her a stunned look. "And now I gotta run a quick errand. You guys okay?" Trish was still tongue-tied, but Fran didn't even wait for an answer. Snatched her jacket, ducked out the back door and began texting the moment she was in fresh air.

Normandie stretched and gave Trish a demented grin. "Man. How much weed did we smoke last night?"

"I guess...quite a bit. At least you did," said Trish, for lack of a better response. "What else did we do? I kind of forgot."

Normandie shrugged. "Hell if I know. Might've been dudes involved, but even that's a big-ass blur. Hey—where's your phone so I can call Rosie?"

"Rosie? Don't you mean...Juanita?"

"Whatever. The phone?"

"Oh! Um...it's kind of not working at the moment. Something with the line."

"Shitskys. Must be the same losers who run the mall." She sniffed one of her armpits. "Man, I gotta shower."

"Sure! I'll um, get you a towel..."

She grabbed one from a linen closet in the hall, walked Normandie back to the bathroom.

"Shampoo's in there. Hot water's usually pretty good. Take your time, okay? And I'll um, get you some sweats you can borrow."

Normandie didn't respond, just stood in the center of the room with her towel, staring at the blue and gold wallpaper and a Disney-esque star and cloud design that was beginning to peel.

"Everything alright?"

"Yah," said Normandie in a hushed tone, "Didn't notice your rad walls before..."

Trish shut the door and scampered back to the kitchen. She disconnected the landline phone, grabbed a stack of unopened bills sporting their Nebraska address, and shoved everything into a lower drawer.

She heard the shower water go on. Trish hurried into her bedroom, opened the chest of drawers and pulled out three or four sets of her sweats. She laid them out on the bed and tried to visualize her guest in each one with mischievous delight. Across the hall, Normandie's sweet, famous voice was singing in the shower. It was the chorus from an old Tom Petty song:

Yeah now, hey hey hey/
I'm a zero from outer space

Trish grinned, then realized something and her face went blank. She peered up at the wall over her bed.

It was still plastered with Normandie Vine posters.

"Uh-oh..."

She hopped on the bed, frantically began taking every one down. Some from earlier in Normandie's career had been up there forever. The tape took strips of the wallpaper off with it, and some of the posters ripped. Trish cursed under her breath, but kept at it.

"Hey, where those sweats be?" yelled Normandie from the open bathroom door. *She was out already?*

"Just a second!!" Trish shook a few pieces of old tape off her fingers, then snatched a random pair of glittery pink sweats, bounced back in the hall and handed them to her.

"Eeeeyew," Normandie said.

"It's all that's clean."

Normandie made a screwy face, grabbed them anyway and shut the door again. Trish raced back into her room to resume poster removal. After sloppily finishing that, she saw that her night table and chest of drawers were littered with an assortment of Normandie bracelets, Normandie keychains, Normandie drinking cups, and Normandie pens and pencils. She ripped off one of her pillowcases and swept everything into it.

Paused when she nearly grabbed a 15-year-old postcard for the Cat Scratchers. It was promoting one of their upcoming shows at the Kearney Community Hall, and there stood Cliff and Jean Dunwoody in their country combo attire, grinning with guitars.

"Hello??" Normandie was out of the bathroom.

"Be there in a second!" Trish leaned the postcard back against the little music box where it was, then quickly carried the pillowcase to the bed, shoved it underneath and followed it with the armload of posters. She stood back up, took a few deep breaths and hopped back in the hall.

"What's shakin', Macon?" Normandie asked, the pink sweats on, her hair sloppily tied up in the bath towel with red hair fireworks shooting out the top.

"Oh...not much." Trish half closed her bedroom door. "How about we hang out in the living room and do our nails or something?"

"Could be rad," said Normandie. Trish led her down the hall with an inner smile, though what Trish really wanted to do was pinch herself. She really did have the younger, non-celebrity version of her idol in her house, and there were so many things she wanted to ask her.

CHAPTER FIVE:
THE COOKIE MONSTERS

Myra Harp's press conference was held in the council chamber room of Eagle Creek City Hall, a modest brick and glass eyesore a block away from the Gift Gulch. The building kept its Christmas lights up year round. At the last moment Myra had listened to her dedicated assistant Howard and agreed to face the press in a more public, lower-altitude place than Peak Experience, though she was severely tempted to stage the event under the treatment center's front door and ruin its reputation forever.

Regardless, over three hundred media personnel had found their way to Eagle Creek, clogged traffic with their vans and satellite trucks and brought the town to a standstill. Chuck and Rashid had come down the mountain, survived another nuclear Harpian tongue- and butt-lashing, and were now standing with their hands folded on either side of Myra and sweat on their thick necks as she addressed the reporters from a podium. A handful of Colorado state troopers and the Eagle Creek sheriff rounded out the entourage.

"Thank you all for coming, media members," Myra began. She was wearing a stiff navy blouse under a bright red L.L. Bean jacket, not too unlike a cardigan sweater on a Komodo dragon. She clearly hadn't slept in days, and had tried to cover the circles under her eyes with a pound of mascara. "I realize what a burden it was for many of you to come here today, but Ms. Vine's disappearance has been a shocking development that has changed all of our lives, and it's important for you to know that we and the authorities are doing everything we can to find her and return her to safety.

"Now before I turn this over to Sheriff Mungo, I just have to say..." She paused for a deep breath, a flick of hand through her faux-spiked hair. "...That it is incomprehensible to me, that a young, beautiful, and endlessly talented woman can go missing from a so-called reputable facility like Peak Experience. I've worked closely with Normandie since she was 13 years old, and while I've never experienced the joy of having children of my own—"

Her voice cracked. A few deltas of mascara began sliding down her cheek. "She may as well...may as well be my own daughter...I'm sorry—"

She left the podium in violent tears, and Howard escorted her into the wings. Patted her shoulder caringly.

"Beautifully done," he said.

"I know," said Myra.

He held up a cell phone. "And I have Tina Blunt for you."

"Who?"

"*Starbrite Monthly*?"

Her eyes freeze-dried on the spot. She snatched the phone out of his hand and walked through a back door.

"Tina, it's been forever."

"I'll say," said Blunt's bemused voice on the other end, "Feel like talking about a Normandie cover?"

"Perhaps. What's it worth to you?"

"We can discuss. But I promise you it'll be Starbrite's biggest seller ever!"

"Hmm. Then I guess it will be worth a lot."

"Sure, as long as she stays missing."

"That's not very nice, Tina."

"I know. But being found isn't quite as newsworthy, is it?"

Something in her pocket chirped. She dug out her personal phone, saw who was calling and made a pained face. "Tina? How about I get back to you tomorrow on this?" She flipped Howard's cell back to him, and put her own phone to her ear.

"Monty Damn Matilda."

"And g'day to you, luv."

"Tell me if I was hallucinating, but I swear I saw you snooping around Peak Experience the other day."

"Hallucination confirmed. How are things in Munchkin Town?"

"Oh, obligatory. To what do I owe the displeasure?"

"Well, me and Delbert been cookin' through the snaps, see? Ones of all the cars parked up in front of that organic fairy castle. And makin' a whole tub of license plate notes. Like Holmes and bloody Watson if you don't mind me sayin'—"

"Get to the damn point, please."

"Well, what I'm sayin' is there's a chance she had a bit of help cuttin' free of that place, right?"

"I don't know. Sounds to me like you're tossing a pretty tiny dart at a big-ass board. I'm sure she's in the woods somewhere."

"Yeah? Far as I've heard, state troopers, locals and half the bloody Sierra Club haven't turned up a thing. Way I figure it, my photo detectiveness could fetch me at least five of them green figures if they lead to where she is...Get me?"

She could practically hear him sneer. "You are one hell of a scumbag bottom-feeder, Matilda."

"I wouldn't live anywhere else, luv. Anyway, isn't findin' Normie quick the biggest food on your plate right now?"

Myra took a long, mind-spinning pause. "How about I get back to you on that?" She hung up on him and kept walking.

*   *   *

Trish and Normandie sat side-by-side on the living room couch, neither of them saying a word. Normandie had a deck of playing cards out and was building herself a shantytown of little card houses on the coffee table. Trish just watched her with a mixture of fascination and anxiety. All of their fingernails were painted fuschia.

"So Amanda," she said, "What should we do?"

"I'm doing it, girl...No rent, free utilities, easy to re-model..."

"Yeah, but I mean—"

"Hey. Got any more of that weed?"

Trish was taken aback, and scrambled her mind for an answer. "Umm, I think maybe we went through it all last night. Don't you remember when we were...singing karaoke at that Chinese restaurant?"

"Uhhhhh...nope. And kind of glad I don't." She looked around the room for a second. "Where's all your CDs?"

"Oh—My dad sold those. And all my cassette tapes. Pretty sure I told you that too at the um, the Peking Rabbit."

"Okay then, wanna watch TRL?"

"TRL. Is that like...a url?"

"A what? No, I mean Total Request Live? On MTV?"

"Aw, I don't think we get that channel on our cable."

"Bummer..."

"Maybe there's some neat old TV sitcom we can watch, though. Like *Friends*."

"Didn't they just renew that?"

"Huh? Oh right! They did. But there's a station that plays old ones sometimes—"

"Y'know? Screw *Friends*. Phoebe annoys me anyway." She leaned over and blew down her entire card village. "Let's go take a walk!"

"No!!"

Normandie stared at her, confused more than anything.

"I mean, we really shouldn't. You had a rough night and it's kind of cold out. W-why don't we just stay inside and bake something and maybe...talk about stuff!"

Normandie stared at Trish like she was from Neptune.

"Bake something?"

* * *

Googy's Market was at the lower end of Endeavor's Main Street, right next to Lucky Laundry and across from Skinner Gas 'n' Oil. Cars and pickups were usually spilling out of its parking lot because Googy Philson was too penny-pinching and cantankerous to expand it, even though her family had owned the property for nearly five decades.

Being the one market in town, it was not only crowded much of the time but a natural community spot for locals, and Googy's father had honored this by constructing a luncheonette counter in the back corner that still had an old fryer and seltzer spigot for making ice cream sodas and "Nebraska Egg Creams." Ranchers were often perched on its counter stools at lunchtime to eat burgers and watch the commodity prices crawl by on the Farm Network, and high school kids filled the handful of tables with their backpacks, phones, and dessert drinks late in the afternoon.

This section of Googy's had been coined the Scoop-a-Loop, which made lots of sense to Fran. She read somewhere that Ben & Jerry's actually began as a health food eatery in an abandoned corner gas station in Burlington, VT, and was originally more known for its homemade lemonade than its ice cream. So why shouldn't a counter that mostly served greasy meat flipped by a greasier dropout named Cyril become famous for its egg creams?

Fran thought of this again while she waited at one of the tables for Dana to show up. She had texted him at least three times, and when he finally responded he was getting into a bath, nearly shorting out his phone in the process. She was tempted to call or text Trish to see how things were going with Normandie, but again, didn't want to risk "Amanda" hearing the chirp of a magic phone device from the future and upsetting her mental apple cart.

So instead she paid a quick visit to the egg cream counter. Cyril was thinner than a shower curtain, had a unibrow between his eyes and a nickel-sized purple birthmark on his neck, but was pretty sweet for a guy and she felt pretty at ease with him.

"Hi Fran," he said. "Medium chocolate again?"

"You got it!"

"What's Trish doing?" He was always asking about Trish, which bugged her a bit.

"Oh, she's...got some homework. Big project!"

"Uh-huh." He grabbed a medium-sized glass, blew inside it and wiped it out with a paper towel. Eyed her a few seconds longer than he was accustomed. "You seem kinda pumped today."

"What's that?"

"Pumped. You know. Stoked about something."

"Oh...yeah. Tried some of my uncle's coffee this morning and it was a little intense."

"You gotta watch that stuff, Fran. I hear it leads to old age." He let out his famous chuckle, which always reminded her of a donkey with laryngitis.

Dana scooted in at that moment, out of breath. Fran waved bye to Cyril and quickly guided her friend to a corner table. He had a macramé scarf around his neck and when he unwrapped it some of the threads stuck in his teeth.

"Spill it, honey. Did you see her? Get an autograph? Been checking your Instagram since you guys left—"

"Better than that!"

Dana finally got his entire scarf off. Raised an eyebrow.

"Really? Snapchat?"

"Uh-uh. Try No. Phone. Needed."

Dana looked bewildered. Fran slid her chair closer to the table, dropped her voice to a notch above whisper. "Listen. What I'm going to tell you is super code red secret. I mean, if someone threw you in the back seat of their car, drove you out to that silo on 59-A and buried you in ten tons of old corn with half of it going down your throat and they wouldn't let you pee for seventeen hours, you still wouldn't tell them what I'm about to tell you. Even if they—"

"What the hell happened, Fran?"

Fran took her sweet time releasing the next sentence.

"She's in our house."

Dana blinked his eyes seven times, without moving his head. Giving Fran a verbal response was definitely out of the question.

* * *

"Those are beyond disgusting."

Trish had pulled a bowl of very old bananas out of the fridge. Normandie was slumped against the counter playing with a strand of her red hair while Trish mashed up the innards in a bowl.

"If you want to make banana bread, Amanda, it helps to have old bananas."

"Isn't it easier to just buy a Sara Lee cake at the store?"

"Sure, but easy's no fun."

"Yeah, but it's easier." They shared a friendly chuckle after a pause. Normandie yawned.

"So where's your mom at? Parents split up?"

"Uhh..yeah. A few years ago. It's been hard."

"Your dad's kind of a studmuffin."

"Thanks. Right...Anyway, you can butter this baking pan for me if you want."

"I'll pass. Reminds me too much of when Lupé got me to help her make taco salad once and I spilled Doritos all over the counter."

"Lupé? Not Rosie? Or Juanita? Actually, at one point I thought you were living with your Aunt Sophie out in Arcadia." Normandie drew a blank, even though Trish had read that tidbit on at least three web sites.

"Naw, that was Lupé."

Trish mopped some perspiration off her forehead and unwittingly glued a big piece of banana gunk to it. "Oh. So your mom never showed you how to cook anything?"

Normandie paused. "Might have. If she didn't kill herself on purpose driving into that tree."

Trish stood there, paralyzed. The banana gunk dropped off her forehead, landed back in the mixing bowl and she didn't even notice.

* * *

As Fran finished recounting the Colorado adventure, Dana finally spoke again.

"Okay. Every lip I have is sealed. But when can I meet her?"

"We'll work something out. Don't worry. For now, though, this is like Fort Knox or Fort Pentagon, got it? Zero access."

At that moment a flock of familiar young voices stampeded into the Scoop-a-Loop. Fran glanced over her shoulder with instant disgust. The Cookie Monsters stood there. Cookie Calhoun, in her trademark ripped mohair sweater, jeans, and spotlessly clean shitkicker boots, took one look at Fran and rolled her eyes.

"Barf parade. Why are you two here? No special ed classes on Sunday?"

"Yuck yuck, and ha."

"What was that?"

Fran flared a nostril at her. "Suck it, Cookie."

Cookie sauntered over to the table. Ran one of her blue-nailed fingers across the top of Fran's egg cream and put it in her mouth.

"Mmm...Good idea." She turned to the counter. "Hi Cyril!" Flashed a large phony smile and rolled over with her entourage to obviously flirt with him. Cookie was famous in school for pulling off a three-week sexcapade with touch football star Newt Worthington before he moved on to Iowa State, and still acted like she was the one who had dumped *him*.

"So are you going to kick her ass or should I?" asked Dana, teeth all gnashed.

"Check it!" said Lakota and pointed at the small TV mounted above the counter. CNN was running video of Myra Harp's news conference in Eagle Creek, the sound muted, but the crawl at the bottom of the screen said everything:

COLORADO POLICE ADMIT
NORMANDIE VINE MAY BE KIDNAPPED

"Schizz-nozzle!" proclaimed Cookie to the entire gathering. "I'll bet the Dumbwoodys are on this like flies on a dog turd!! Though knowing them, they'd probably settle for just the turd."

Her minions hooted. Fran and Dana ignored her. Cookie grabbed a straw and blew the wrapper-missle at Fran's head. "Am I right, Dumbwoody? All over this? Making plans to head for the Rockies with your butterfly net and find her yourself?"

"Good idea," said Fran. "Knock yourselves out."

"What was that?"

"She said GET BENT, YOU WITCH," barked Dana. Cookie knocked the double egg cream out of his hand, splashing some of it in Fran's lap. Fran shot off her chair, cocked her little fist, but Dana grabbed Fran's arm from behind.

"Don't waste a punch, girl. She's got like seventeen witch spells. One even hacks your phone."

"Oh baby oh baby," returned Cookie. "Already peeing my pants."

"Thought I smelled something," said Fran, who wiped the egg cream off with a clump of napkins and tossed them at Cookie. "Let's bail."

She headed for the exit, dragging Dana with her. "Have fun in Colorado!" yelled Cookie, the Monsters giggling around her.

* * *

Fran never ran so fast in her life. The day was unexpectedly warm and dry, parched her throat with every breath, and the quick-melting snow caused her feet to land in unseen puddles on the side of the road. Even worse, Cyril's darn egg cream was turning her stomach into a Cuisinart's blend setting.

The moment she reached Poplar she saw Trish scoot out on the front porch to greet her—less winded but equally anxious. Fran wasn't sure, but she thought she heard rock music coming from somewhere.

"Thank God," blurted Trish, "I almost texted you but didn't want to take out my cell phone because you know why—"

"Tell me you don't have the TV on."

"What? No, no. That's just Normandie—I mean Amanda. And you won't believe the stuff she's been telling me! First of all, her mom didn't lose control of her car on a wet road. She actually killed herself! And she has so many maids she says are picking her up I can't even keep their names straight—"

"You left her alone in there?"

"She's fine. Is something wrong?"

"Well, the cops in Colorado are now using the word kid and the word nap, and not in a pre-school kind of way. Plus the Cookie Monsters just watched the news with us."

"Oh cripes."

Normandie let out a yelp from inside. Fran flew into the house, Trish on her heels. They recognized the pounding rock beat right away. It was an oldie even their uncle knew, and assorted friends of their had occasionally called up the song's creepy YouTube video. They rounded the corner into the living room and stopped, because

Amanda/Normandie had donned a dishwashing glove, ripped off the fingers, and was perfectly lip-synching to Billy Idol's "Dancing with Myself" while she gyrated around the room.

"CD?" Fran asked Trish.

"Uh-uh. Classic rock radio in Kearney."

If I looked all over the world
And there's every type of girl
But your empty eyes seem to pass me by
And leave me dancin' with myself.

"Should we do something?" asked Trish.

"Like what?" said Fran.

Too late. Their guest shoved back the coffee table with her foot, grabbed both of their arms, yanked them into the center of the room and got them dancing. Trish turned beet red and looked more out of place than a Queen's guard in a mosh pit, but made the most of it.

CHAPTER SIX:
SNOWBALLING

Dave sat in his clinic office, trying to place an online order for Acepromozine but kept entering the wrong codes or misspelling the word.

Patty popped her chubby head in. "Yesterday's mail, Doctor! Just got to it now."

"Um...okay."

She entered, plopped a rubber-banded clump on his desk. "Will Farquahr is back with Bob, his ferret? But he doesn't have an appointment. What should I tell him?"

"Probably...to make one, right?"

"I tried. He said you gave him a full checkup last time anyway."

Dave pulled off the rubber band, leafed through some bills and pieces of junk mail. "Maybe because no one else was scheduled, or it was a holiday. I don't remember..."

He got to a couple of magazines for the waiting room: *Cat Fancy*, *Travel and Leisure*. The next one in the stack was the new issue of *People*. Normandie Vine's exploding red hair and groggy face stared at him beneath a garish headline: WILL NORMANDIE EVER LEARN?

Dave leaned back in his chair, gripping the cover in his hands. He was suddenly unable to breathe.

"Huh," continued Patty, "because I checked and we just have the Yandles and their Corgi in a couple hours. I was actually thinking of ordering in Rico's Tacos and we could have 'em out on the patio. Y'know, if it's warm enough—"

"No! I mean, no thanks. Not all that hungry..."

Her face sagged a little. She started for the door.

"To tell you the truth, Patty, there's something I need to take care of all of a sudden." He hopped to his feet. "Maybe you could finish ordering the Acepromzine for me?"

"Sure!" She turned, color suddenly in her cheeks. "Is everything—"

"Yeah. Plumbing. I mean, there's a plumbing problem at the house. Not sure the girls can handle it. Be back soon—"

He threw his jacket on over his doctor coat, dropped his car keys twice before scooping them back up and bolted from the office.

* * *

Dave wheeled his Volvo onto Poplar Avenue, skidding on the slippery road a few yards. As he pulled into the drive, nearly hitting their mailbox and then the old Focus, sweat was pouring down his cheeks. He jumped out of his car, noticed that a pillowcase had been draped over the Focus' Nebraska license plate. He started for the kitchen door and stopped.

He could hear girl-laughter and occasional squeals coming from behind the garage. Jacket unzipped and snow swallowing his nice work shoes, he hurried around the back and a round white projectile whizzed past his ear.

"Sorry!!"

Words couldn't even sputter out of him. Normandie, Trish, and Fran were having a full-blown snowball fight, every inch of their hair, faces and clothing covered in icy white patches.

"Us against them, Mr. D!" yelled Normandie with an exuberant, devilish grin, "How about it?"

"Not right now. Trish? Fran? Can I speak to you a minute?"

"I didn't mean to buzz your face just now, Mr. D. Seriously—"

"I realize that Amy—I mean, Amanda. Girls? Please??"

Trish and Fran dropped their newest weapons and trudged across the yard to him.

"Holy shit—" uttered Dave, the moment Normandie was out of earshot. "What have you two done?"

"About what?" asked Fran, futilely playing dumb.

"What is Normandie Vine doing here??"

"SSH!" blurted Fran, dropping her voice. "We're helping her. You wouldn't believe the awful treatment she was getting in that organic hell-hole."

"Right," added Trish, "Scandalous."

"So you actually drove to Colorado?"

"Right," said Trish, "To show our support, you know? We made up all these signs in the garage—"

"It's just the next state over," added Fran. "Not really that far—"

"And then we couldn't get near the place. And we turned around to leave—"

"We didn't even use a credit card or anything for gas or food—"

"And she crawled out of the woods all messed up, definitely from the treatment, and dragged herself into our back seat when we weren't looking—"

"That's right," cried Fran, "Of all the thousands of fans who were there, she picked us to rescue her! Isn't that the coolest?"

"No. It's nuts. They're probably looking for her everywhere! For God's sake, we're harboring her!"

Fran calmly shook her head. "She's not a fugitive, Uncle Dave. She's just a lost girl. Like one of those pets people bring to your clinic all the time, right?"

Dave was at a loss for words again. Glanced over at Normandie, who was busy building herself an armory of fresh snowballs.

"So...why is she calling herself Amanda?"

"Because that was her real name," said Trish. "Until she was 14."

"Amanda Mushnik from Chatsworth, California," continued Fran. "I know. It sucks. I mean, even I would change that—"

"Okay. But where does she think she is?"

Trish and Fran shared a pause before Fran took the lead again. "Some place out near L.A. called the Grapevine. It's up this Route 5 freeway through some mountains. We figure she had a friend or two there. And that it had snow sometimes. And now, excuse me a sec—"

She yanked another pillowcase out of her snowjacket's pocket, ran around the back of Dave's Volvo and stuck it over his Nebraska plate.

"Well, there aren't exactly any mountains around here," continued Dave. She is going to figure this out—"

"Yeah, but she's also still kind of high," said Fran, hurrying back and lowering her voice even more. "See, she had her own drug stash up at Peak Experience. Klonopin. I Googled it and asked Dana, who's sort of a drug expert—I mean like a hobby—and it definitely can cause amnesia. So...we think it did. Gotta figure she'll probably be whacked out like this for at least a few days, right?"

Dave gave them a resigned nod. He knew about Klonopin. "Great. Okay. So in the meantime, I'll make a few calls, let people know where she—"

"NO NO NO!" Trish and Fran bark-whispered the word in unison, and so loud that it made Dave jump. Normandie glanced over at them for a second, but was still distracted with her icy armaments.

"No what?"

"We can't do that, Uncle Dave," said Fran, "These places they've been sticking her? These treatment centers? They're terrible."

"Depressing!" added Trish.

"Didn't you tell us that Mom and Dad always said to think before you jump? Or something like that? Well, believe me, we've been thinking this one from the second she fell into Mom's car. And the best thing for her right now is a nice, quiet place where she can chill."

"And be herself."

"Even if she thinks she's 14?"

"Well," said Fran, "it's probably more like 12, to be honest—"

"But with two of her most loving, caring fans in the world!" Trish's eyes were filling up. Fran put a firm, cold hand on Dave's wrist.

"She really needs us..."

"NO FAIR MAKING BATTLE PLANS, DAD!" yelled Normandie from across the yard. Trish groaned. Dave nearly keeled over.

"Did she just call me Dad?"

"Yeah," said Fran, under her breath. "Just go with it. It's easier, believe me."

Dave threw up his hands. Stared off at the naked, creaking trees a long moment. "Okay...So tell me what happens when her people discover where—"

"They won't!" said Trish, as certain as she'd ever been about anything.

"Not unless we rat her out," said Fran. "And we are never gonna rat Normandie out, right?"

"Gee I don't know, girls. Do you really think—"

"Just for a couple of days then!" said Fran in a rush. "Until she can relax a little, and y'know, spend some time not being judged for once. I mean, look how happy she is already."

The three of them turned to look over, just as a new snowball zipped through the air, exploded on Dave's upper chest, and popped a few hunks of snow into his gaping mouth. The girls broke out in laughter. Spitting out the snow pieces and wiping his face clean with his jacket sleeve, Dave managed to crack a tolerant smile.

None of them noticed Meg Strump, who had been watching the entire snowball fight from the front window of her house.

* * *

On the other side of the world, in a quaint Italian village carved into the side of a small mountain, an extremely tanned and fit man in his 50s sipped cappuccino at an outdoor café. He wore dark glasses, an expensive Versace shirt, and white slacks over a pair of handmade leather strap Roman sandals. He had an issue of *la Repubblica* open on his table beside an unopened *Wall Street Journal*.

A headline in the Rome newspaper suddenly caught his eye and he sat up to re-read it. Over a standard Normandie Vine concert photo were the bold words:

STAR AMERICANA: PERSO O RAPITO?

The man's lips tightened. He gulped down the rest of his cappuccino in one sip and extracted a cell phone from his slacks. Quickly speed-dialed a number and spoke very capable English to whoever answered the call.

"Sorry to wake you, but I need a phone call made, please...Yes. To Stuart Fine at Morgan Stanley in New York...He can reach me here..."

He signaled to the waiter for another cappuccino, who was on it in seconds.

"Oh, and one other phone call please…" He drummed his fingers on the white tablecloth for a moment. "To Lawrence Wilburton at the U.S. Department of State."

CHAPTER SEVEN:
MAIN STREET U.S.A.

Dave pulled into the parking lot of a Runza Sandwich, killed his engine, but wouldn't leave the car right away. Two Nebraska state troopers were exiting the eatery toting plastic Runza bags, sharing a joke while they climbed into their cruiser a few spaces away. One nodded in Dave's direction, and Dave mustered enough courage to nod back, though his hand was on the Volvo's door handle with a good mind to jerk it open. Trish and Fran had good hearts, sure, but was keeping this celebrity in their home the smart thing to do? If she was discovered there and the consequences were bad, couldn't it put his vet practice in jeopardy?

After a few more moments the troopers pulled out of the lot without Dave racing to their window to spill any beans, and his body relaxed, his latest anxiety gone for the time being.

Inside the restaurant minutes later, he stood in a short line and gazed up at the menu board in a fog. He had contemplated getting something to go from Googy's or Rita's Tacos, but wasn't sure how cast iron Normandie's stomach was, so after leaving Poplar Avenue in a hurry he shot down Route 73 a handful of miles to the Runza chain at the brink of the interstate.

"Next guest, please!"

The quandary now was exactly what to order. Was Normandie vegan? No, she was putting that bacon away earlier like no one's business. But was that just the teenage Normandie appetite?

"Next guest??"

He snapped out of it and approached the counter. Found himself looking at an awkward high school girl with a full mouth of braces. "Yes, hello. This is to go. I'll take one original Runza—actually make that two, a Swiss and Mushroom Runza...and um...What are your salads?"

"They're all on the board. Right side."

"Ah yes. Okay, and a Chicken Bacon Ranch Salad. No wait. Make that a Southwest Chicken Salad. We uhh... have someone staying with us from the west coast, you see."

The girl faked a smile. "Any drinks?"

"Um, no. Actually—do you have any imported bottled mineral water?"

"Any what?"

"Never mind. Thank you." She began ringing it up. Dave stood there in a new trance until the girl had to tell him the total a second time.

* * *

When he got back to Poplar Avenue, the girls were in the house again, had changed into dry clothes, and were listening to the same classic rock station in giddy delight. If anything, Trish and Fran seemed to have regressed in age. Fran was smiling and laughing more than Dave could remember, while Trish was busy entertaining Normandie with an antique photo album from the Dunwoodys' turn-of-the century days.

"Got Runzas!" announced Dave from the kitchen. The trio whooped and rushed in. Within minutes, Normandie had helped set the table and poured them all too much soda.

"I was truly not ready for that fastball in my neck, Fran!" she cried, her face still flushed from the Thirty Minute War.

"Shit flies at you every day," said Fran, "Gotta learn when to duck."

"Well, I want a rematch A-S-A-Possible."

"It's a date."

Normandie dished out a movie villain laugh and plopped into Jean Dunwoody's memorial chair again. Dave began to say something, then caught himself and put what was left of the giant soda bottle back in the fridge.

"Well, these look hell-a-yum. Thanks, Dad!!" said Normandie, and grabbed half a sandwich off a serving plate.

"Oh," said Dave, "I got you a sal—" Too late. She took a huge bite, then paused when she noticed everyone looking at her. "Whoopsies.

Are we supposed to drop a grace bomb here? Because I don't remember one at breakfast."

"No...Amanda," replied Trish, "I think it's more like a manners bomb."

Normandie took the hint. Leaned back in her chair and waited. The second Dave's bottom hit his chair she grabbed her Runza again and went to town on it. After the second bite she let out a passionate squeal.

"Heaven better have a food court that sells these puppies, because I have just died and gone there."

Someone rang the doorbell. Trish, Fran, and Dave shared a panicked glance.

"Oh!" yelled Normandie, "That could be Juanita!" The girls were too paralyzed to respond. Dave got up and gingerly walked to the front door.

"Can I help you??"

"I come in song!" shouted a familiar teenage voice on the other side. Dave was mystified. Trish and Fran instantly recognized one of their booster club's code-sayings, though. "It's Dana!" cried Trish.

Dave swung open the door and Dana shot inside like he had Tabasco sauce in his boxers. He walked straight into the kitchen, gave them all a rapid wave, and fixed his eyes on Normandie.

"You're...Amanda, right?"

"This is our friend Dana," said Trish, "He just found out who you—I mean, that you were here from out of town—"

"Hi!" Dana put his hand out. Normandie high-fived it nonchalantly. Dana looked at his blessed hand a long moment, then back at Normandie. His grin was so wide his teeth resembled piano keys.

"You hungry?" asked Dave.

"Uh, no. But that's cool!" He continued to awkwardly stand there, unsure what to do with himself or any of his limbs.

"I got us Runza sandwiches," said Dave.

"No that's okay."

"There's more than enough, Dana," said Fran.

"Naw, I'm good."

"Sit the hell down, dude!" yelled Normandie, and Dana abruptly dropped on a nearby footstool as if the Hulk had screwed him into it.

"Actually, I am kind of hungry," he said, randomly snatching half of a sandwich off the serving plate and dripping half of it on his jeans. Normandie squinted at him.

"Were you at the sleepover last night?"

"The what?"

"You know!" cried Fran, trying to sneak a wink, "The party I told you about that we all got a little zonked from?"

"Oh! Right! No, I missed that. But you can fill me in later... So Amanda—how long you in town for?" The sisters shot him a perturbed look. "Today, I mean."

"Got me," said Normandie, her mouth full of Runza, "I'll split when someone picks me up, I guess. Assuming someone gives a crap."

"Oh, I definitely give a crap. Many craps." Dana rocked his footstool across the floor until it reached the table. "Why do you think my friends in school call me Captain Craptastic?"

"They do?" asked Trish, wincing at the pint of cologne Dana had apparently poured on his neck.

"That's pretty high-larious," said Normandie.

"It's really my new nickname," continued Dana, "Guess what my old one was."

"Prince Deludo?" muttered Fran.

"No, it was Brown-Eyed Boy. You know, like a spin on that old Van Morrison song?"

"I don't know who you're talking about," Normandie calmly said. Dana cleared his throat and badly sang:
Youuuu my...brown-eyed boy

"See?" he said, pointing at his muddy brown eyes.

"How could you not have heard of Van Morrison?" Dave carefully asked Normandie. "Just curious."

"Aw, I don't bother with music before 1990 unless it's the Rolling Beatles or someone. It's kind of like me and really old movies like

Rain Man. They put me to sleep."

"Tom Cruise was pretty hunky in *Rain Man*, don't you think?" chirped Dana, "He's like the same height as me—"

"Any more Coke Zero?" asked Trish, jumping up from the table out of sheer panic. Fran was having a hard time taking any further bites of her sandwich.

"Like I said, I was 40-winkin', so I probably missed hunky Tom."

"Well, I'm up for a part in our school play at the moment," resumed Dana, "And I know I could act that nerd off a cliff—"

"O-kay!" exclaimed Fran, "Amanda's still a little beat from last night, so we kind of have to do an early evening."

"But I just got here—"

"Bye Dana!" said Trish, "See you at school!"

"But Dalton just got here!" said Normandie, "And I'm ready to freak!"

"Err. It's Dana…"

"You *think* you are, Amanda," said Fran, ushering Dana to his feet, "But trust me, you're not. Last night's gonna hit you like a rock 'n' roll wall."

"Take care, Dana," said Dave, "Thanks for stopping—"

Fran was already out the front door with him. Normandie looked at Dave and Trish with a cute, pouty expression.

"I liked that little dude."

Out in front, Fran hurried Dana down the steps and practically tossed him back on his bike.

"This isn't fair," said Dana, "I barely got to talk to her."

"I think you talked enough. You didn't even text us that you were coming, Dana. And what's this school play garbage? The school doesn't even have a theater class!"

"Yeah, but she didn't know that!"

"Listen. Our uncle's being pretty cool about this, but we only get two days with her before she has to leave."

"That's all?"

"Exactly. Meaning as long as she thinks she's Amanda, every

second of time we can spend with her gives us a better chance of straightening her out. Didn't you notice how happy and fun she was? Before you started blabbing at least?"

Dana began sputtering another blab.

"Zip it, Dana. Don't even try. Listen...We'll find a way to squeeze you in again, I promise, but in the meantime, please keep all of this to yourself, okay? Loose lips crash cars and all that."

* * *

An hour and a half later, Amanda gazed dreamily at herself in the Dunwoodys' bathroom mirror. She may have been standing there for twenty minutes, but her sense of time wasn't exactly reliable lately. All she could imagine was how skunked she must have gotten at that sleepover the night before. Her hair was still frightening and a strange color, and there were practically shopping bags under her eyes. It was almost as if she had aged fifteen years.

Why do I always lose control so easily? Rex and Fabrice and T.T. are always so good at getting blitzed after sixth period. They're even great at holding on to their vomit. Trish and Fran and their teddy bear dad are nice and all, but Sofia will track me down one of these hours and get me home and into a hot bath and POOF—more new friends kicked to the stupid curb...

"Amanda? You okay in there?" It was Trish's voice, forever concerned.

"Yup! Think that Kwunza sandwich did kind of a number!"

"Okay...Anyway, it's your turn! You just got married!"

Normandie took a deep breath. Turned and flushed the toilet for show before exiting.

Milton Bradley's *Game of Life* was spread out on the living room floor, and as banker, Dave was making the cash piles neater as Normandie re-entered and dropped to the rug between Trish and Fran.

"Anyone knock me up yet?"

"Hey, good question," said Fran, half-sarcastic.

"Have to spin the dial to find out," added Dave blandly. Trish and Fran had suggested playing the game to use as a possible Amanda fact-finding mission, and weren't sure if he still realized that.

"Not that anyone will ever try," said Normandie, as she spun the big dial in the center of the board and moved a couple of spaces. "Oh man. 'Eccentric aunt leaves you 100 cats. Pay ten grand to give them away.' I love cats! Can't I just keep them?"

Fran chuckled and spun the wheel. Moved five spaces. "Damn—another baby daughter? I can't fit any more kids in my car, y'know. If I get another one can Amanda just adopt it?"

"Very boss of you," said Normandie, "but I don't want no stinkin' kids."

"You have to take one if the game gives it to you, Amanda," said Dave, giving the spinner a healthy whirl.

"And if you don't have any you have to give $50,000 to an orphanage if you land on that orange space," added Trish pertly.

"Well, screw that," said Normandie, "Who wrote this dumb game anyway?"

"It's actually the classic edition from 1960," said Dave. "My older brother found it at a yard sale. And...y'know....gave it to us."

"They got some more modernized versions you can get onli–I mean, buy in stores," said Trish, "but we always play this one."

"I mean, look at this stuff!" said Normandie, "Buy a yacht? Pay 500 bucks for a new set of choppers? What the heck are choppers??"

Trish was afraid to say anything else, spun the dial and moved six spaces and whooped. "Yeah! 'Inherit cattle ranch, collect $102,000'! Hand it over Pops." Dave handed her the money with a grumble. Normandie spun the wheel again, moved, and her face froze.

"Alright, you got a baby daughter!" exclaimed Trish. When Normandie still didn't react, she grabbed a little pink child peg from the box and stuck it in the back seat of Normandie's car.

"Presents!" announced Dave, and each Dunwoody handed her a $500 bill. Normandie just stared at the tiny plastic vehicle on the board. Her eyes were glazing over.

"At least nobody was in the car with her..."

Trish and Fran exchanged glances. Dave gave Fran a friendly tap on the arm. "Your turn—"

"SSH," whispered Fran, leaning in closer to Normandie. "You're talking about your mom, right?...Her accident?"

Normandie's entire mouth stiffened. Her eyes remained foggy. "I was eight...Third grade...but I knew how much booze and coke she could put away..."

Dave let out a small nervous laugh, then wisely clammed up. A chilly hush filled the room.

"At first I thought someone was in the car with her but nope...She was alone...Then I heard Dad on the phone with some guy. A month or two later...There was white powder all over the seat. All over her nose..." After another spooky, withdrawn moment, Normandie gave her hair a comforting toss. "So who's turn?"

The game awkwardly resumed. Like he usually did, Dave was winning handily, making investments, gambling successfully. Millionaire Acres was engraved on his little blue car like it had a GPS. They made it unscathed over the toll bridge, though Normandie's money was visibly dwindling, and two spaces away from the DAY OF RECKONING spot on the board, Normandie's hand suddenly froze on the spinner.

"Amanda?" She didn't respond to Fran at all, her attention wandering this time to the living room window. Poplar Avenue's two old streetlamps had come on, and she could see a few dead amber leaves fluttering off Meg Strump's tree. Lights had appeared in each quaint little house, giving the neighborhood a warm, archaic glow.

"My dad took me to Disneyland that weekend...like it would cheer me up..." She managed a weak chuckle. "Nothing did but Main Street."

"Main Street USA?" asked Trish. They'd heard of that place, but confined to Nebraska their entire lives, it may as well have been on another planet.

"I wandered away...He had just bought me an ice cream cone and I wandered away. Walked into one cute little fake house after another...There were nooks...and there were crannies...and finally found a back hidden stairway and went up to a room that wasn't being used for anything...like it was part of a movie set you only saw from outside..."

Dave had been quietly counting one of his phony cash piles to distract himself. Lost his train of thought and laid the pile down, folded his hands and just listened.

"Stayed up there the rest of the day. Sometimes peeked out the window and saw Dad freaking out, Disney security people on their walkie-talkies trying to help him...

"Weird thing's that I felt so safe...Like as long as I could stay upstairs on this cute little fake street, nobody would find me or bother me...I could actually get old there." She pointed out the living room window.

"You got your own Main Street right here, y'know...All these cute little houses and friendly people and nothing to make me nervous. I mean, I know we're at a high elevation on the edge of the California desert and stuff, but I could move to this street in a second and never leave."

It was so quiet you could hear an Adam's apple drop.

"Well..." said Dave, groping for anything, "It certainly is a nice little town."

"So what happened?" asked Fran, "I mean...When did they find you?"

Normandie's eyes were filling up a bit. She wiped them dry with one of her fake ten dollar bills and shrugged.

"Sometime after dark. Disney people put me in a room and tried to grill me, like I heard they used to do with hippies, and I probably would've been arrested if my dad didn't barge in and yank me out...I think he felt bad for leaving us and moving to Chicago, and that weekend he was in town and doing the overprotective thing big time." She stared at the little white plastic mansion for Millionaire Acres at the end of the game's road, then at the slightly smaller gabled house four spaces back labeled POOR FARM. "Sometimes I still miss him..."

Her fingers were getting sweaty atop the spinner, and she

suddenly recoiled from it. "I um…need to go lie down a while." She stood and went down the hall to Fran's bedroom.

"So…" said Fran, a little distraught, "I guess you won again…*Dad*."

Dave nodded silently. It was by far the least joyous victory playing Life he'd ever had. "Think she's okay?" he asked.

"I think she will be later," said Fran, who stood up and began to pace. "I mean, this was some heavy stuff people don't even know about."

"Really? Her mom's accident wasn't reported?"

"Not that way," said Fran. "Not as a suicide. Or that she was high on cocaine and booze and who knows what else."

"And that day she had at Disneyland!" cried Trish, "Geez…I feel so much more bad for her than I did before."

"If only she could just stay Amanda," said Fran, "Even when she leaves, so people could see how sweet and wounded she really is." The girls glanced at their uncle, almost for confirmation. Dave methodically removed each of the child pegs from his car.

"No doubt that must have been tough," he said, "to lose her mother like that." He took a long moment, then quietly finished putting the game board and parts back in the box, and walked across the room to slide it back in a cabinet.

"Meantime," resumed Fran, "I bet there's more stuff she can tell us."

"About what?" asked Trish.

"About anything. Maybe there's like a secret clue that sort of explains her. Why she took such a turn for the worse later on."

"Right. A clue like the one they had in that old Orson Welles movie, remember? Rosemead!"

"We need to make sure she has fresh towels and bedding," said Dave, starting for the hall.

"On it!" proclaimed Fran.

"Can we put her in my room tonight?" asked Trish. "Fran got her last night."

"But we didn't even talk! She was out of it. You guys made banana bread. One more night and then you."

"No way. I drove all the way to Colorado and back, so I get her tonight."

Dave just shook his head from the hall. Fran made a big farting sound with her lips in Trish's direction.

"Oh, okay. Big fat deal."

Down the hall, Dave saw Fran's bedoom door open a crack and peeked inside. Normandie was curled on the bed, snoring away. He stared a few extra seconds. Beneath her wild hair she really did have an awful pretty face.

* * *

An hour or so later, after Normandie had woken again and groggily made her way into the bathroom to wash up, Fran armed herself with some fresh towels and knocked on the door.

Normandie opened it, her hair pinned up and soap all over her cheeks.

"Yeah?"

"Hi again…Amanda."

"Uhh…Hi."

"Just checking to see if you need anything else."

"Nope. I'm cool."

Fran continued to stand there awkwardly. "I don't mean to bother you. It's just pretty remote out here. Meaning we don't get a lot of house guests, so—"

"Remote? We're only like an hour from L.A, right?"

"R-right, but it's still pretty quiet most of the time, especially when we start getting snow."

"Hear ya." She finished wiping off her face and making it radiant again, even without makeup. Turned back to Fran. "Anything else?"

"Huh? Oh no—except here's some fresh towels."

Normandie smirked, opened the door wider to reveal another set of fresh towels, already sitting on the edge of the sink.

"You gave me those ten minutes ago, chick-o-rina."

Fran blushed, smacked her forehead with a free hand. "Wow. Fail. Old age sneaking up on me!"

"Ehhhh not quite yet." She winked and closed the door. Fran took that as a compliment, stayed in the hall to deep breathe for a second before walking away.

* * *

Trish had blown up a mammoth air mattress, arranged it on the floor beside her bed, and dressed it with flannel sheets, two comforters, a handful of her favorite stuffed animals and a half dozen cozy pillows. She had changed into her *Bug's Life* pajamas after sneaking a search on her phone to make sure the movie had been released when Normandie was still Amanda.

When Normandie entered the room wearing Trish's favorite new nightgown, a bright red number featuring two sleeping puppies and the slogan "Don't Quit Your Daydream", Trish just about melted into a giddy puddle. Then she noticed Normandie gaping at the air mattress.

"Oh! Hope this is okay for you, Amanda. I get real bad backaches when I sleep on it, otherwise—"

"So it's okay if I get one?"

"Oh, I don't think you will. You're in much better shape than me and all."

Normandie climbed into the thing, which she practically needed a stepladder for. "Probably won't matter. I feel like I could sleep for a week."

"Hey—you sure could if you wanted to." Trish got in her own bed and made herself comfortable, naturally, on the side closest to Normandie.

"We have got to get out of here tomorrow. Gettin' a little bit stir crazy."

"We'll figure something out," said Trish, without any idea what that would be.

Normandie laid on her back, and let her eyes dart around the dim room. "Hey...How come you don't have any stuff on your walls? You should come down to my place sometime and check out my concert posters."

Trish's eyes popped open in horror, suddenly remembering all the Normandie Vine stuff she had stashed under the bed. She rolled slightly on her side and carefully peeked below. Normandie's right elbow was maybe a foot away from one of the folded-up posters sticking out from under the dust ruffle.

"Best one I got is from a Ramones and Social Distortion show at the Greek Theater—"

"Hey Amanda?"

"Huh?"

"I've just been thinking about it, and it feels weird that I'm up here and you're down there. I mean—you're our guest and really should have the comfier bed."

"What about your back?"

Trish was already climbing out and motioning for Normandie to swap with her.

"Oh, I can swing it for another night. Took an Advil like an hour ago for a headache and it usually helps my back, too. My bed is so, so comfortable, so...go girl!"

Normandie was too fried to even contemplate it, let alone argue. She struggled out of the air mattress creation and slipped into Trish's bed.

"Much more comfy, right?" The words were three seconds out of her mouth and Normandie was snoring. Trish fought her way under the air mattress covers, paused to shove the Normandie posters even deeper under the bed with one of her hands, and switched off the bedside lamp. She took a deep breath, realizing that there were at least five more fact-finding questions about their house guest's past she didn't get to ask her.

"Good night, Amanda," she whispered to herself, "Whoever you are..."

* * *

Somewhere off a Colorado interstate, Monty Matilda's mini-van was parked at the far edge of a Holiday Inn parking lot. Tumbleweeds, sagebrush, and a bit of trash blew across the dark, mostly unoccupied lot, and seemed to part for a rented economy car that suddenly came speeding into the space alongside the van. Delbert killed the headlights, climbed out toting a plastic shopping bag, hurried over to the van's side door and knocked twice.

Monty slid it open. He was shirtless, sipped from a can of Foster's and had some Japanese speed metal blasting.

"Bingo, brother!" shouted Delbert.

"Did I just hear a 'bingo'?" yelled Monty, dropping the music volume by half.

"I didn't say 'dingo'."

Monty grinned, moved aside and let Delbert hop in. Slammed the door shut.

"Beer?" Monty asked his young protégé.

"Nope. Your VHS still work?"

"If I can find the dusty old bitch, definitely." He stepped over to a giant leaf pile of cables, connectors, broken tripods, dead routers, and other electronic garbage taking up space in the corner. Tossed everything aside with both paws and yanked an ancient VCR out from underneath. Blew off the grime on the top and front and plugged it into an extension cord for a portable generator that was charging his laptop and at least four other devices.

"Right. What you got?"

Delbert eagerly opened the plastic bag, handed him a VHS tape marked LULU'S COUNTER / PUMP 4. Monty popped it into the VCR, switched on a little monitor.

"Figured I hit up over 25 gassies before that one. Had a mind to skip it but lucky me, had a bad case of the trots."

A fuzzy, wide-angle shot of the place's counter came up. Maybe a couple of truckers in line buying beer. Nothing special.

"Them?"

"Hold your petticoat, mate." The image jumped ahead fifteen minutes, on Fran, buying her Red Bull and giant bag of Skittles. "That one!"

"Her? She's an ankle-biter!"

"She bought Normandie Vine's favorite snack. In bulk. And see that? Runs out right quick after looking up at the TV screen."

"Yeah? Maybe she don't like Oprah."

"Just watch."

A camera view of gas pump number 4 followed. The image was still a bit fuzzy, but they could clearly see Trish leaning over a sleeping young woman in the back seat of their Focus as a slightly amped Fran arrives and they drive off in a hurry.

"Right? Now hurry up and do your magic, so I can go use the gents room and brush my teeth," said Delbert. Suddenly electrified, Monty went to work on the VCR's buttons. Back and forth, back and forth, frame-by-frame employed. Finally stopped on a decent view of the Focus' rear Nebraska license plate: YK5 6P3

"Pass me the laptop." Delbert quickly grabbed it off the floor, handed it to him. Monty clicked on a photo library, dozens of shots snapped in and around Peak Experience the day Normandie disappeared. He zeroed in on ones of people and parked cars on the road leading to the entrance. Stopped on what looked like the same color Focus and zoomed in on the car's front license plate: YK5 6P3.

"Hand me my cell, you wonderful bastard."

* * *

Myra's phone went off on the night table in her suite at the Ritz-Carlton Destination Club in Aspen. The vibration was so violent it knocked over her empty martini glass and shattered it on the hardwood floor.

She cursed herself awake, peeled off her sleeping mask and lunged for the phone. Exhaled painfully when she saw who was calling.

"Waking me up is a felony in 48 states, Matilda."

"Then I'm guilty, luv. But don't hang up this time."

"You have five seconds to enlighten me."

"Only need three. Got a license plate, and a location."

Myra sat up, lowered the phone a moment to let this sink in.

"You're positive."

"Delbert paid for a gas station video tape. Plates match a car in front of Peak, and Christ if you can't see her in the back seat."

"Tied up?"

"Could have been. Who knows what these bastards are doing to her."

"So on the tape you can...see the bastards?"

"Kind of, yeah. Was a couple of young bettys actually, but my guess is they delivered your girl to either a meth gang or an extortion ring. Happens every day down in Columbia or Mexico, right?"

For once in her life, Myra couldn't even respond.

"Suppose this location of theirs will be worth a lot to you then?" asked Monty.

"No, Matilda...In fact, I'll wire you a nice check in a week or so if you keep this under your big floppy hat."

"I don't wear a bloody hat."

"You know what I mean. I got a half dozen editors and TV producers foaming in their pants for drama. The longer we milk this thing, the bigger it could get for all of us."

"Except Normandie ain't exactly a cow. And in a bloody week she could really be in Columbia or Mexico—"

"So find where she is, Matilda. And keep her on this side of the border please."

CHAPTER EIGHT: HITTING THE FAN

Twelve Poplar Avenue on Monday morning was a friendly Midwestern madhouse, or as Dave occasionally said, "like one of those TV comedies where people are always coming in the front door." He had let Trish talk him into letting her take a school sick day to "Amanda-sit" again. Fran, already annoyed over Trish winning this precious right, was more distracted than she usually was getting ready for school.

"You put my backpack somewhere Trish. I know you did."

"Why would I do that?"

"Because you're older than me and think you can do anything."

"Didn't we just talk about this? You can have Normandie after dinner, okay? And she can sleep in your room again tonight for all I care."

"Oh, that's a big old har har. You sure damn do care—"

"Girls!" cried Dave from his room, right on cue. He had his own issues, because Patty at the clinic was a little under the weather and really hoping to leave before noon, and Dave knew that there were at least three dog appointments and a guinea pig scheduled.

"Don't forget, one more day learning what you can about her and tomorrow we're making that call."

"We know, Uncle Dave," grumbled Trish in between Pop Tart bites as they criss-crossed in the hall.

"And you're sure you've got this today?"

"Well, I did okay with her yesterday. She sleeps till like one in the afternoon, and Fran will be getting home a few hours after that. We'll be fine."

She went to the kitchen. Dave stood there, a bit out of sorts. Began to zip up his down jacket and realized he had it on inside out. He yanked it off, then saw that the door to Trish's room was open slightly and peered in again.

Normandie was curled up on her side but the bedcovers had been kicked off. The bottom of Trish's red nightgown she was wearing had bunched up a smidgen, revealing black panties and a little bit of pale butt crack.

"Ready to go??" It was Fran from the kitchen. Dave quickly shut Trish's door, sorry he had just seen that, and ashamed he had looked as long as he did.

*　*　*

Ten minutes later, Dave meandered his Volvo around a few idling cars to the front walk of the school. Fran was deep in thought, and in no hurry to get out.

"Really hope Trish stays focused on her car accident thing. Always been a mystery to us why Normandie suddenly went from straight arrow to druggiehead, y'know? It's not like she had a traumatic relation—"

"You got your backpack?"

"Yeah...Know what I mean, though?"

"I suppose. Except those sound more like Normandie questions than Amanda ones."

Fran half-turned in the passenger seat with a resigned look.

"One more day's better than none, I guess..." She started to climb out, then leaned back in and gave her uncle a kiss on the cheek. Dave smiled and took that in for a moment before driving away. He never got those.

*　*　*

At home, Trish peeked into her room. Normandie was now completely facing the other direction, legs tangled in the bedcovers. She was still asleep, her steam valve snore back in force, but her mouth moved slightly as though trying to shape words. Trish thought she heard one and tiptoed closer.

"Don't know you Rex..."

Trish's eyes widened. The steam valve returned, and she grabbed a pen and sticky note off her desk. Scribbled REX. She inched close to the bed again.

"No..." Normandie muttered, "You're mistaken..."

Trish was suddenly four inches away from her face.

"MISTAKEN!!!"

It was louder than a Doberman bark, and knocked Trish backward. She slipped and nearly crashed into her dresser, catching herself on a chair.

"Wanna see Paula..." muttered Normandie, before she rolled over and the steam valve morphed into a grinding, drawn-out latte machine. Trish quickly made her way back to the hall and shut the door, her mind racing.

Paula again...No Juanita? No Rosie?

A new thought came to her. She went to the kitchen door, grabbed her hoodie off a wall rack and hurried out to the garage. Virtually all of the fresh snow had melted, and she had to hop over a few slushy puddles getting there.

Inside, she switched on the overhead light and went to a far corner. Dusty canvas covered a shadowy, three-foot-high shape. She pulled off the canvas, revealing two giant plastic tubs. The top one was labeled with magic marker on masking tape:

NORMANDIES (AGE 13-16)

* * *

Ms. Stewart, Fran's mousey world history teacher who was all of 25 years old but also very smart and from Winnipeg, was talking about the Renaissance. Nearly half of the twelve kids in the room were listening and taking notes, a fairly good ratio, but Fran couldn't be bothered this time. She and Dana sat at opposite ends in the second to last row, texting each other behind their propped up textbooks.

Fran: T. WANTS ME TO ASK U WHO "PAULA" MIGHT BE
Dana: IDK. OLD VOCAL COACH? ACTING TEACHER? PERSONAL TRAINER?
Fran: BIG HELP

Dana: HEY I'M JUST A FAN. NOT A DATABASE.

Ms. Stewart had reached the Russian architecture portion of her Russian portion of her Renaissance lesson. To Fran it seemed like she'd been on this topic for over a month. Vince Fasher a few seats away had perfected the art of dozing with his eyes open.

Dana: WHAT IS TRISH DOING WITH HER?
Fran: LITTLE AS POSSIBLE I HOPE. WHEN NV'S AWAKE SHE'S LIKE A PARAKEET TRYING TO GET OUT A WINDOW.
Dana: SO TOMORROW WHO WILL YOUR UNCLE CALL FIRST?

Fran thought a bit before answering. The very idea of Normandie leaving made her clammy. Dana was as patient as he could be, but was itching to know, and didn't realize that Heather Zim, one of Cookie Calhoun's more scheming little Monsters, was sitting in the last row behind him, peering at the texts on Dana's phone and trying to make sense of them in her miniature brain.

Fran: GOT ME. COPS OR MYRA OR PEAK EXPERIENCE. THEY ALL SUCK.
Dana: YA. MAYBE THE 3 OF US CAN JUST TAKE HER BACK ON A BUS.
Fran: WHAT R U SMOKING? OH—T. JUST ASKED IF WE'RE HAVING ANY LUCK. TOLD HER YOU NEVER HEARD OF NO PAULA. AND TO KEEP ON LOOKING FOR OUR "ROSEMEAD"
Dana: ROSE WHO?

* * *

In the garage, Trish had pried open the top plastic tub. The thing was a treasure trove of clipped-out newspaper and magazine articles, each one with a recurring theme:

"Normandie is Reader's Choice Again!" (*Teen Scene*)
"Vine Shines in 'Locker Days' (*Chicago Tribune*)

"Normandie Vine Cancels Salt Lake Gig Due to Flu" (*Salt Lake Tribune*)
A ten-year-old copy of *Billboard* sported a screaming front page headline:
"BUMP" GRINDS VINE ATOP POP CHART
with
VINE DEBUTS 15-CITY EUROPE TOUR
adorning a special pull-out section.

Trish kept digging through the clips, which seemingly had no end to them:
"Normandie Too Busy for Boyfriends"
"Normandie in Rehab Again: Will Three Be the Charm?"
"New Vine to Die For"
"Stormin' with Normandie"

The amount of press the girl received was intoxicating, and Trish drank herself silly on most of it, smoothing out each clipping and being unable to put it back without reading a few paragraphs. Time seemed to evaporate whenever she went through these tubs; she couldn't even count the weekend afternoons she and her sister had lost themselves.

* * *

Back in Trish's room, Normandie grumbled and turned over. Squirmed and turned over again. Somehow her body told her she had to pee and she slipped out of bed, eyes half closed, and staggered out to the bathroom.

"What's that?" she whispered to herself, or to whoever was still in her half-concocted dream. "What's that in your hand?..."

Somebody somewhere rang a doorbell.

"Hello?...You better get that..."

It rang again, a little clearer this time. She finished peeing, realized the bell may have been real, and made her way down the hall to the front door. She fumbled with the knob a second, then opened it on Meg Strump, all apple-cheeked in the crisp air despite the third morning cigarette hanging from her mouth.

"Oh! I was looking for David. His sidewalk could use a bit of shoveling."

Normandie managed a sleepy smile. "Really? You got me up for that?"

Meg flashed a frown, but seemed more curious than anything. "So you must be their out-of-town guest. I'm Meg."

"Right. Yeah. Amanda…"

"Oh! Funny, but you know something? You are a dead ringer for the missing celebrity girl. The one that disappeared from that fancy health ranch in Colorado the other day?"

Normandie went numb and pure white, like an alluring pillar of salt. Meg didn't even notice.

"Oh, what was her name? Norma something…"

"Normandie…" The words weren't even a whisper, more like a sun-dappled brush stroke on Normandie's lips. Her eyes were beginning to deepen again.

"That's right. Normandie Vine! Anyway, silly and goofy me, I suppose people tell you that all the time, don't they? Have a good day, hon—and tell David to shovel!"

Meg ambled back down the steps. Normandie wanted to move, but somehow couldn't. She rotated her eyes and then her head, until she could see down Poplar Avenue. Slowly turned and looked the other way. Then felt something odd about her body, dropped her gaze and saw she was wearing someone's bizarre red nightshirt.

A little U. S. Postal jeep rounded the corner at that moment, pulled up to each mailbox on the street and began filling them. Normandie's eyes telescoped in on the jeep's NEBRASKA license plate.

"No effing way…"

She shivered, stepped back inside and closed the door. Put her back to it. Gazed around the house with a jumpy, panicked expression.

"Hello??"

No one answered. November wind rattled a windowpane, and something creaked in the attic. She left the front hall, began moving from room to room, looking everywhere for something.

"They took it...THEY TOOK MY DAMN PHONE!"

She opened cupboards and drawers in the kitchen, every compartment in the bathroom, under the mattress in Dave's room.

"Where are you, baby?...WHERE DID THEY PUT YOU??"

If Normandie wasn't so angry she would have been sobbing. She darted back through the kitchen and entered the den. Froze when she saw the television. She glanced around, saw a sloppily-hidden remote sticking out from under a stack of blankets. Grabbed it, aimed it at the TV and began pushing buttons. The power came on but the input source changed and all she got was loud snow.

"Damn it!"

Her button-pushing got wilder. Finally, out of sheer luck, she landed on live TV and began channel surfing. Stopped on CNN, where Myra Harp was being interviewed by two women on a national daytime show and trying to beat back invented tears.

"Colorado law enforcement has been wonderful. No rock or tree or creepy abandoned cabin for fifty square miles around the facility is being overlooked. Normandie's fans have been flooding social media with their good thoughts, wishes, and prayers. Someone's even started a Twitter account called Vine Vines, which are nothing but continuous loops of her best concert and screen moments running 24/7..."

Normandie's mouth fell open. Her entire body shook, swayed. She flung the remote across the floor, then let out an unearthly, livid howl and kicked over a wooden crate beside the couch. Wool blankets fell out, along with a small pile of DVDs. She looked down at them a second, then crouched and grabbed a few. *Locker Days, the Complete First Season. Vine in the Rhine: The German Concert, '09.*

"What the shit..."

Normandie peered up at the bookshelf beside the TV—and two completely empty shelves. She yanked the blankets out of the crate and dumped the other twenty DVDs on the floor.

"You creeps…"

She left the den, crossed back through the kitchen and down the hall. Opened the door to Fran's room and stepped inside. The walls were tastefully decorated with macramé, some old hippie beads and a framed, vintage black-and-white photo of John Lennon by Annie Leibowitz. Normandie had a weird, sudden thought—like a flash of odd lightning still in her head—and closed the door, moved instinctively down to Trish's room.

Trish's walls were completely empty. In a few places, there were still pieces of double-stick tape. She opened the closet and saw only clothing. Checked a few drawers on Trish's dresser and came up with nothing unusual. Started to leave again and noticed something protruding from under the bed. She dropped on her knees, hauled out one hastily rolled-up poster after another. The motherlode of Normandie Vine kitsch.

"You…creepy…MONSTERS!"

She dropped the posters and bolted from the room. Halted again in the kitchen, her ears perked. Somebody was singing…

In the garage, Trish was halfway through the second plastic tub of Normandie material and the second verse of "Baby Makes Me Wanna". Normandie, wearing Trish's ridiculous pink bunny slippers, stood just outside the double doors, listening to her. She was shivering in the cold, but had worked herself up into a livid lather and didn't exactly feel it. She glanced around.

A few feet away was a green trash barrel on wheels. Normandie went over and peeked inside. It was still filled with wet leaves—heavy, wet leaves. She grabbed it from behind, tipped it forward and carefully rolled it over the snowy driveway to the garage doors. Wheeled it around and found a way to wedge it firmly between the garage's door handles. Smirked at her handiwork for a moment, then went back to the house.

Inside, she cruised by the den again. The Myra Harp interview was over, but now there was a breaking news item, superimposed over one of her hit album covers:

$150,000 REWARD OFFERED FOR
NORMANDIE VINE WHEREABOUTS

"The reward money is reportedly coming from an anonymous source, possibly in Europe," said a newscaster. Normandie just stood there at the entrance to the den, gazing at the screen in a fogbank. Her face twitched a little, like she was on the verge of a stroke, before she turned, zombie-like, and walked slowly back through the kitchen.

Found herself in the bathroom again moments later. Shaking now, she opened the medicine cabinet and rifled through three or four prescription bottles for DAVID DUNWOODY. Nothing she could use. Distraught, she began opening drawer after drawer under the sink. Stopped when she saw a pair of scissors.

Back in the garage, even Trish had her limit when it came to poring through Normandie clips; two and a half plastic tubs were enough. She did find a couple of interviews in teen pop magazines that mentioned "Aunt Sophie in Arcadia," but found nothing revelatory, certainly nothing about her sudden plunge into drug abuse in the last five years. As far as she could tell, a broken romance didn't even seem to figure in.

Trish neatly folded the two interview clippings, then closed and re-stacked the plastic tubs in the corner and returned to the garage door.

It wouldn't open.

"What the heck?..."

She pushed on each side individually. Neither would budge. Frustrated, she laid the magazine clippings on the floor and rammed her shoulder against the double doors. All that did was hurt.

"I cannot believe this."

* * *

Dave and Patty had just given a mild sedative to Twirp, the Poston family's pet Myna, and Dave was preparing to apply a bandage to the bird's crooked leg when his cell phone vibrated once on a table across the room. Patty looked up for a moment.

"Number three scissors please..." said Dave. Patty was clearly distracted by the phone sound, and hesitated. "Patty? You with me?"

She nodded, passed him the scissors and Dave snipped the bandage in place like a diamond cutter. Over on the adjoining table, the text message from Trish read I'M LOCKED IN THE GARAGE!

* * *

The exact same text also lit up Fran's cell phone, on the dark shelf inside her gym locker. Fran and Dana were busy outside "running the perimeter", which consisted of following the entire circumference of the cold, windswept school grounds in their yellow gym shorts and tops without passing out. Fran and Dana tended to fall to the rear of the pack in no time, and suddenly even Lizzie Koosh jogged past. Lizzie was a gangly physics whiz unafraid to attend school wearing a headgear to support the metal alloy factory of braces in her mouth.

"Hey Fran...Where's your sister today?"

"Uhh, home sick."

"Too bad...She must be all watching the news then!"

"News?"

"Yeah...Normandie Vine reward money. It's like a million dollars or something. Aren't you guys her biggest fans?" She started to blow past them.

"Lizzie! Where'd you hear that?"

"Cookie Calhoun! Blabbing about it in the hall right before gym!"

Fran and Dana exchanged an anxious look and actually picked up speed.

* * *

Trish wasn't sure how she was able to lift two of the plastic tubs herself, but it was too late. She had, and now gravity was kicking her butt. Braced against her uncle's workbench for a moment, she gathered momentum, transformed her 17-year-old body into a battering ram and smashed the tubs into the garage's double doors. The impact knocked her to the floor and tumbled the tubs on top of her, but one side of the doors had been forced open. She got to her feet, wedged herself between them and managed to kick the barrel of wet leaves away.

She was in the house's back door seconds later.

"Amanda?"

There was no response, but she could hear the television on in the den. She went to the doorway, didn't see Normandie, but the TV was tuned to CNN coverage of THE SEARCH FOR NORMANDIE.

She left the den, paused in the kitchen. Saw Dave's cash container empty on the counter.

"Uh-oh...AMANDA??"

She hurried down the hall, noticed the Normandie posters lying in a heap on the floor of her room. Panicked, she ran back in the hall, catching something in the bathroom out of the corner of her eye. She swung the door fully open.

The sink was filled with Normandie's red hair.

* * *

At the Aspen/Pitkin County Airport, the Harp Worldwide Management private jet taxied onto the runway. Myra was comfortably buckled into her plush leather seat with her first Bloody Mary of the day when her cell phone rang. She groaned and answered.

"Make it quick, Howard. We're about to take off...No, I was taking a mudbath, why?"

Whatever he said next turned her expression to molasses. "How much and from who?...No, Howard. No donor is ever anonymous." She hung up, furious.

"Moroni..."

The plane turned around on the runway, ready for takeoff.

"GAVIN! DON'T TAKE OFF YET!"

A few yards away in the cockpit, the grey-haired, seasoned pilot glanced over his shoulder. "Everything okay, Ms. Harp?"

"Yes and no."

The pilot frowned, looked at his equally puzzled co-pilot a second. "We have a new destination, Ms. Harp?"

She took a healthy swig of her Bloody Mary.

"I'm thinking."

* * *

At a clothing factory on the outskirts of Istanbul, the tanned, silver-haired gentleman we last saw at an Italian café shook hands with the overweight but impeccably groomed factory owner.

"Once again, it is a pleasure to do business with you," said the owner in Turkish.

"It certainly was," said the gentleman, also in Turkish, "Excuse me a moment—"

He took out his cell phone and walked a few paces away. Read a new text on it and smiled.

CHAPTER NINE:
OVER THE TRACKS

S hivering with a blank expression, Normandie walked down the
  icy sidewalk into town. She still wore Trish's bunny slippers and
had donned one of Dave's plaid wool jackets, but it wasn't close to
being warm enough. She had cut a good deal of her hair off, and
secured the choppy mess under a pink and navy ball cap from
the Nebraska Pork Guild. Having also re-donned Trish's purple
sunglasses, the last thing she resembled was Normandie Vine.

The descending sidewalk was rather treacherous, and a couple
slippery patches nearly pitched her into a snow bank, but she
somehow regained her balance and kept moving. Her eyes darted
around the frozen town, like a fox expecting a farmer with a shotgun
at any moment. Words tried to escape her mouth, but the few that
did were unintelligible.

Endeavor Square appeared on her left a few blocks from the
center of town. Its collection of bench, two cottonwoods, broken
water fountain and plaque for town founder Delbert Boggs covered
in bird crap looked more forlorn than usual, but Normandie noticed
the skanky guy in the watch cap seated on the bench right away. And
made her way over.

He was in his late 20s and had a dangerous drifter quality to him,
but Normandie was very familiar with the type and acknowledged
him with a nod.

"Yo. Got anything?"

The guy shrugged. "I dunno. Like what?"

"Oh, c'mon. You know…"

"No I don't."

She gave the guy a little nudge. "Out of towner. So do you or not?"

He looked her up and down—mostly down, at her wacky slippers.

"Got a few buttons. Fifteen for one, twenty for two."

"Buttons?"

"Mandrax, baby. Imported from South Africa. Make you feel good all over."

"Oh. I used to call those whites."

"Yeah, whatever. Got the cash? Won't get a better deal down on Main Street."

She gazed at him, her eyes weirdly brightening.

"Main Street?"

"Yeah. You want 'em or not?"

She re-focused. "Let me see 'em first."

"Uh-uh. Let's see your cash."

She turned slightly, reached into the clump of bills in her jacket pocket and extracted a twenty. The dealer glanced around, then pulled off his watch cap and produced a tiny plastic bag with two white pills inside. They made the exchange and Normandie started to walk.

"Hey," the dealer said, "You can mix those things with tobacco or weed and smoke 'em."

"No need," uttered Normandie. She was already chewing on one.

* * *

Ms. Mendez was busy writing an algebra problem on the board, so didn't notice Fran slip into the room with her backpack and drop in her seat. Fran was still sweaty from gym class, and very harried. Dug out her cell phone and saw it was out of juice.

"Damn it..."

Ms. Mendez whirled around at the board. "So you've joined us after all, Franny. Super. Was something wrong?"

"Oh yeah. The homework was impossible this time. Was working on that last problem in study hall and totally lost track of time."

"Good. Keep at it!"

Fran gave the teacher a canned smile, waited until she turned to the board again, then dug in her pack and extracted a phone charger cord. Fran's seat was inches from the window, and after opening the textbook and biding her time until Ms. Mendez surveyed the room again, quickly dropped to the floor and plugged the phone into a wall socket under the window. It made a goofy "power on" jangle and Ms. Mendez whirled yet again, but Fran was already back in her seat and diligently copying the new math problem off the board.

"Phones OFF please!" said Ms. Mendez tiredly, having said it about 1,748 other times in the first three months of the school year. While Fran sat with the phone on her leg beneath the desk, waiting for it to come to life, car tires screeched somewhere outside. It was Trish, peeling into the student parking lot in the Focus. Moments later, her I'M LOCKED IN THE GARAGE! text appeared on Fran's phone.

"Okay! Who can tell me what the Order of Operations is?"

Fran stared at the text, then glanced out the window again. Baffled.

"Fran? The Order of Operations?"

"Uhh—sure. It's the order you...do operations in."

"Good guess. Give us an example."

"Well...for instance...If you—"

The intercom box atop the blackboard buzzed, and a crackly, officious voice from the school office popped out.

"FRAN DUNWOODY TO THE OFFICE...FRAN DUNWOODY..."

"Whoops, gotta go!" exclaimed Fran, yanking her charger cord out of the wall, collecting her things and fleeing the room in one motion.

In the front office, Trish was pacing around with two uptight assistants eyeballing her as Fran entered.

"Can you believe Dad's car?" said Trish. Slides off the road into a ditch!"

"Golly! Are you kidding?"

"He's okay, but we should really get down to the hospital, you know?"

"Oh, you bet!"

Fran scribbled her name on an excusal form and they bolted for the exit.

Old Jeannie was parked at the end of the front sidewalk with two of its wheels up on the curb.

"Nice job," said Fran.

"Be quiet and get in!" yelled Trish, "Why didn't you answer my five texts?"

"Phone was dead! What happened—"

"She's gone."

"Amanda?"

"Worse. Normandie! Somehow she got up and put on the news, I think, then found all the DVDs and freaked the heck out and cut off her hair!"

"No. Not her hair!!"

Trish nodded and they screeched out of the school lot.

"She's on foot, thank god, so probably hasn't gotten far."

The Focus careened around the corner and headed into town. Neither of the sisters noticed a figure in a ball cap, plaid wool jacket and purple sunglasses making its way across a vast, snow-covered field behind the school.

Normandie was wobbling, already in a Mandrax cloud. She kept her bloodshot eyes glued to the snow patches her bunny slippers were trudging through, softly muttering to herself.

"Main Street..."

A bell rang from the school. Like a drugged mare she turned slightly and followed the sound. The bell was for the end of the school period, and three slacker-looking students came out a back door, propped it open with a book bag, lit up cigarettes, and began laughing hysterically at someone's joke. Normandie exited the snowy field a few yards away and wandered into the school with the three kids barely noticing.

The hallways at Bill Baird were especially teeming between Second Period and First Lunch. Normandie, in her odd outfit, received a few curious glances, but managed to glide straight down one of the corridors in her semi-trance state. Students swerved around her, hurrying to the cafeteria or next class. Every slamming locker gave her a needed jolt that kept her moving forward.

She entered the cafeteria. Her purple sunglasses had fogged up, and she raised them. Saw the students grabbing trays and lining up at the food counter. Frowned and sided over to an elderly battleaxe of a cashier.

"Chuck and Rashid…"

"Hah?"

"You seen Chuck and Rashid?"

The cashier waved her away. Normandie stood there a lost second, then dropped the sunglasses on her nose again and drifted back to the hall.

She followed two yakking girls into a restroom, which was five times more packed and noisy then the corridor and filled with cigarette smoke. The foul air got to her instantly, and she tried to evade it by walking into an empty stall. Her vision obscured by the sunglasses, she banged off the toilet and concrete wall behind it, and the sunglasses dropped into the unflushed bowl. Grimacing, she slid out of the stall again and weaved to the restroom door.

Heather Zim swung it open, nearly colliding with her. There was a flash of recognition for Heather, like seeing an actor in a scene she couldn't quite place, but then it was over. She grunted an apology and Normandie slipped past. The door swung shut. Maybe it would come to her later, but dang! Who *was* that??

A warning bell sounded. Dana came racing around the corner and up to his locker. He spun the dial and looked up to see Normandie drifting toward him, every slamming locker making her jump. With the purple sunglasses gone, Dana recognized her face immediately.

"Amanda?"

She looked at Dana but nothing registered. Dana quickly swapped out a book, shut his locker and backpedaled down the hall alongside her.

"You okay? What's with your hair?"

The corridor was thinning out. Normandie pointed a finger groggily at a far exit. Dana peered down and saw the bunny slippers.

"Holy crap, aren't those Trish's? Hey—lemme take a quick selfie!"

Dana yanked out his phone, dropped his pack and threw an arm around Normandie. She was blasted out of her mind, but even her distant unconscious knew what a selfie was, and she leaked out the shred of a grin as Dana snapped it. The moment the phone was re-stuffed in his back pocket, Normandie slipped free and continued out the exit door and into the snow.

"Cool. See you later, I hope!" Dana knew something was wrong with her, but he was late for his next class. He would text Trish and Fran the photo from there.

Meanwhile, Heather Zim remembered who that weird girl in the restroom looked like, had watched the selfie being taken, and was already moving rapidly up behind Dana.

* * *

Trish drove the Focus through the center of town, Fran hanging out the open passenger window and scanning every alley and piece of sidewalk.

"Did you try Maple Street?"

"We were just there!" said Trish.

"No, that was Elm Street."

"I don't care if it was Oak, or Birch, or Cottonwood, or Weeping Willow. We've covered like every tree street in town."

"Maybe she got picked up at the house while you were stuck in the garage."

"I told you. I wasn't stuck, she barricaded me! And who the heck is going to pick her up? Endeavor Uber?"

"Forget this. Just go back up the hill…"

Minutes after the Focus drove away, Normandie stumbled out of an alley in the center of town. She paused to dwell on a sign for Main Street, then peered around and was instantly saddened by the scarce, shabby storefronts.

Then she spotted Police Chief Gilmore across the street, waving to a passing trucker. Normandie instinctively ducked back in the alley and calmed herself with a few deep breaths.

"Wrong Main Street...Wrong one..."

She carefully peeked out. Chief Gilmore was strolling toward the upper end of town. Normandie waited until he was about a block away, then snuck around the corner to Butchie's Hardware and entered the store.

Butchie, the elderly owner in his suspenders and butch haircut, was dozing behind the counter with a comics section in his lap when Normandie jingled the bell on the front door.

"Howdy-do there!" he said, wriggling to his feet.

"Hi. Can I get a bus to L.A. around here?"

"You mean Los Angeles? Well, gosh darn. Pretty sure you can't, miss."

"How about the Valley?"

"Valley?"

"San Fernando..."

"Never heard of that one. Maybe someone down at the Broken Burro knows." Normandie looked lost. Butchie came out from behind the counter, scratched his cheek, and pointed out the window to the lower end of the street. "Over those tracks."

The Broken Burro was a sad, squat excuse for a bar, fifty yards or so past the last remaining Endeavor building, a tiny impromptu junkyard, and across a set of train tracks that led in both directions into prairie infinity. Normandie half-staggered over them, nearly tripping on each rail, the saloon's demented-looking neon burro over the door and faint accordion music like multi-sensory beacons.

Two young Latino women in frilly blouses, jeans, and high heels got out of a dented Subaru in the Burro's pickup-packed dirt parking lot and clopped their way in. Normandie peered at them for a groggy moment, then picked up a little speed and entered the place behind them.

The Burro was mainly a boisterous, smoky migrant worker's bar, with some unafraid local ladies sprinkled in. Norteño music poured from a juke box in the corner, floppy rancher hats and dirty cowboy boots were the fashion staple for men, and about fifteen of them sat or slouched against the bar with their *cervezas*, leering at the two women and Normandie as they entered.

In her normal state Normandie may have been terrified, but the Mandrax had locked her in a trance, and now she was focused on the older of the two Latino girls, who was a little overweight but had a sweet face, silvery lips and was snapping gum inside them. Normandie tapped her on the shoulder a few steps from the bar.

"Sofia! Why didn't you call me?"

The girl turned, looked Normandie up and down.

"Excuse me?"

"I've been stuck here for days and you never called…"

The girl issued a scoffing laugh, turned back to her friend. "Take a walk, *mujer loco*."

Normandie didn't move, her eyes filling with even more imaginary hurt.

* * *

Trish drove past Endeavor Square on their way home. Fran glanced over and spotted the local dealer, comfortably back on his bench.

"Shit. Turn around."

"Huh? Why??"

"Just do it!"

Trish sputtered, but slowed the car and began turning it around.

"You said she got into Uncle Dave's cash stash, right? We haven't looked over the tracks yet."

"Hey, Normandie has issues, but she isn't the type to cross the tracks."

"Unless she wasn't exactly Normandie."

Trish let that sink in, but her foot was already down on the gas pedal.

* * *

Inside the Broken Burro, the Latino women had taken a small table with their Coronas, but hadn't shaken Normandie yet. A snappy salsa tune came on the juke box and she wobbled up behind her chosen role model with the sauciest expression she could muster and laid a hand on her shoulder.

"Dance with me, Sofia...It's been forev—"

She swatted Normandie away. "Don't touch me, freak! And I'm not Sofia!!"

Normandie stumbled back, nearly pitched over an empty chair. Then the jukebox song heated up and the rhythm weirdly began to stabilize her. Her hips swayed. Two of the migrant workers set their beers down and ambled over from the bar.

"You want a good salsa lesson, chiquita?" asked one, looking a bit too drunk to provide what he promised.

"Two lessons!" blurted his friend. Normandie's eyes darted around, as if suddenly realizing where she was.

"Uhh...think I'll pass."

"No way, chiquita. First I make you pass out!" The two men began pawing her.

Outside, Old Jeannie bounced over the train tracks and passed a small homeless camp in an alley.

"See her?" she asked Fran.

"Nope."

They spotted the Broken Burro just up the road.

"Worth a try?" asked Trish.

"Sure. Except we're underage."

"The heck with that. Family emergency, right?"

Inside, Normandie was being passed around on the Burro's small dance floor between three migrant workers. She looked freaked out, possibly nauseous. The two Latino women remained at their table, enjoying the macabre show.

Trish and Fran opened the saloon's door at that moment, as gunslinger-ish as they dared to be. Normandie saw them and her face turned chalk white.

"NO!!!" She yanked herself away from the creepy workers, raced for a back exit. Trish tried to run after her but the workers blocked her path with their sloppy salsa dancing. Fran had a hunch, tore back out the front.

Got in the parking lot and spotted Normandie huffing her way toward the tracks.

"Normandie, wait! We're your friends!!"

"Bullshit! Stay away!"

Fran was in much better condition, closed in on her after just a few yards. Then a low sound shook the ground and she slowed up to look left.

A freight train out of Denver was rumbling straight toward them. Blowing its horn—with Normandie completely oblivious.

Fran broke into a mad run. Normandie heard, then saw the train. Tried to beat it across the track but tripped on the first rail and fell between two of the ties. The engine was twenty yards away. Normandie tried to get back up in a daze but wasn't going to make it. Fran dove at the last second, grabbed her ankle, pulled her back off the tracks and lay on top of her on the dusty ground.

Trish raced up behind them, horrified. Crouched and waited with Fran and Normandie for the endless freight cars to roll past.

"We got you, Normandie..." Fran whispered in her ear. "We got you..."

* * *

Dave hurried out of his office and hopped in his car. It was 4 p.m., an hour before he usually left the clinic, but worry had gotten the best of him again. First, after treating cat fight wounds on both Peanut and Jelly, the Gorkys' feisty longhairs, he had overheard a waiting room customer talking about the huge reward being offered for Normandie Vine's whereabouts. Then in the last ten minutes he had gotten around to seeing Trish's text on his phone about being trapped in the garage. Which is why he was now leaving her a message while he backed out of the lot like a wild man.

"Trish, it's Uncle Dave! Did you get out? I hope so! Just saw the text that you e-mailed me, and I'm on my way home. Okay bye."

He ripped through the center of town, taking a chance on Chief Gilmore wagging his finger at the car if he saw it. When he pulled into the driveway on Poplar, the first thing he noticed was the Ford Focus, parked at an odd angle in front of the half-open garage. He climbed out, propped up the plastic barrel of dead leaves lying in the snow, then stuck his head in the empty garage a moment before heading for the kitchen door.

He entered mayhem. Trish and Fran had a flustered Normandie in the den, Fran trying to keep her on the couch while Trish stood in front of the television, clutching the remote to her chest as if it were a sacred dagger.

"I need to know…" said Normandie.

"No you don't!" said Trish.

"No one tells me what to do."

"Except us, Normandie. Right now—"

"Could someone tell *me* what's going on?" yelled Dave, surprising them.

"Yeah, you're a bunch of kidnappers!" growled Normandie, too stoned to even fight Fran anymore. Trish quickly took Dave's arm and ushered him from the room.

"She knows, Uncle Dave."

"Knows what??"

"Who she is! I have no idea how it happened, but Amanda's gone, and Normandie with all her problems is back, and—"

"Alright then. That's it. I'll call 9-1-1, and we'll turn her over."

"No—"

The doorbell rang. Dave started to answer it and Trish beat him to the knob. Opened the door on a completely frantic Dana.

"Is she here? You got her?"

"Yeah, Dana. It's all good—"

"'Cause she was at the school! We even took a selfie and I was gonna text it but then I lost my stupid phone—"

"Hey! I said it's good. Talk to you later, okay?" She closed the door on him, turned back to Dave to retrieve her thoughts. Her uncle had taken out his Nokia.

"I'm doing this," he said, and flipped it open. Trish threw a hand on top of his and closed it.

"No! I mean—not yet, okay? She's a mess in there! Can't we just keep her a little longer?"

"For chrissakes, Trish, she's not E.T.! She's a troubled famous person who should be under professional care—"

"Right, and that's why we brought her here. It wasn't professional—"

"OKAY!!"

This outburst was from Fran, releasing her hold on Normandie and jumping to her feet. She had yelled so loud it startled them, and had even captured Normandie's fragile attention. Fran stood there in the center of the room a prolonged moment, hastily gathering her thoughts.

"It's been a real chore the last few days keeping appearances up, but now I think we'd better clue Normandie in."

Dave and Trish shared a befuddled look. Fran quickly turned to Normandie.

"Trish, Dave, and I are actually professional de-programmers. And we were hired privately by a large group of your fans to um, ease you back into the world after your harrowing stay up at Peak Experience."

Normandie squinted at Fran through her mind-haze. "Large fans?" Trish and Dave were equally squinting.

"Right! It's called, um, the League of Loyalists. The LOL, for short."

"The LONL!" corrected Trish, "The League of Normandie Loyalists. And Dave here is the head caseworker."

Dave began to form a harsh reply and Trish nudged him in the ribs.

"Oh..." muttered Normandie, semi-coherently.

Fran crouched in front of her. "I bet you're not even aware of the PAVs—y'know, psychological abuse violations—that place has been racking up."

"In the hundreds!" piped in Trish.

"Yeah," said Dave, "Except our de-programming contract is expiring today, so we should probably make other arrangements—"

"Really?" said Fran, hurrying over to him. "I just talked to the main LONL office a few hours ago, and they said they'd be happy to give us an extension."

"Well, that's not what I heard."

"No, Dave," said Trish, "I heard that too."

"Who did you talk to?" asked Fran, "Mr. Garfield or uhh...Taft?"

"I don't remember, so why don't we call them again right now just to verify?" Dave opened his phone again, punched in 9-1-1 and headed into the kitchen with Trish and Fran on his heels.

"I think they're closed for the day!" barked Fran.

"They never close," said Dave. While he tried to distance himself from his nieces by walking back and forth around the kitchen cutting board, Normandie rose off the couch in a fresh distressed trance, and walked unseen to the back door.

"Garfield said they were closing at noon!" pleaded Fran. Trish heard an odd bang and glanced around at the open kitchen door. A gust of wind had just knocked it against their recycling basket, apparently. Or had it?

"Guys?"

They turned together and looked into the empty den.

Then they heard a loud splash from outside.

"NORMANDIE!"

They raced out the door, into the backyard...

Normandie had thrown herself face-first into the pond, and was floating lifelessly away.

"Oh God! We've killed her for real!" shouted Trish. Normandie was sinking into the leafy bog. The girls stood there, helpless. Dave instinctively yanked off his jacket, started untying his shoes. He dove into the frigid water with one of his shoes half off. Swam a few yards. Dove under, got a grip on Normandie's arm and pulled her back up. Trish and Fran went to the edge to help him haul her out and lay her on the snowy grass. She looked dead.

"You know CPR, right?" Trish asked.

"Yeah...A long time ago at summer camp but—"

"DO IT!"

He tilted her head back. Hesitated.

"Was it two one-second breaths?..."

"HURRY!!"

He put his mouth on Normandie's. Blew once. Then again. There was no response.

"Do the other thing!" yelled Fran.

"I know! Have to get exactly between her..."

He sat on top of her, positioned his hands in the center of her chest and gave it one quick pump after another. Normandie still wasn't responding.

"We have to call 9-1-1 now—"

"DO THE MOUTH AGAIN FIRST!" screamed Trish.

"Can I?" asked Fran.

"No, no. I got it." He clamped onto her lips once more. Did three massive breaths and Normandie coughed a pint of pond water into his face. Gasped for air a few times until her lungs were slowly back to normal, then gazed up at Dave like waking from a bad dream.

"Whoa..."

Her teeth chattered. Trish had already run in the house and returned with a blanket, and the girls helped sit Normandie up and wrap her in it. Dave sat on the grass beside them, winded and also shivering. They had forgotten to bring a blanket for him.

* * *

A few hours after dinner, a thrown-together medley of leftovers, Dave stood at the kitchen counter, pouring hot water into a pair of teabagged cups. Fran was quietly collecting the dirty dinner dishes when Trish came down the hall from her bedroom.

"Well, she remembers jumping in the water, at least." She looked at her uncle. "How's that going?"

"Fine. It's not like I haven't made tea before."

"Want us to help bring it in?" asked Fran.

"No, I got it. I'm sure you guys will do a great job cleaning up." He smiled and took the two cups down the hall.

Normandie was resting in Trish's bed. She had showered and donned another one of Trish's nightshirts. Dave set her cup down on the night table and she gave it a wary look.

"What's in it?"

"Herbal tea, just like the girls promised. Good ole' orange spice."

She managed a weak smile. Her chopped hair resembled rhubarb pie.

"Feeling a little better?" asked Dave.

"I guess. There's only so much scummy pond water you can spit up." She eyed him. "So I know I was whacked out on white buttons before, but I swear I heard you guys mention you were some kind of deprogramming professionals?"

"Right. Exactly. The League of Loyalists—I mean, Normandie Loyalists." She kept a deadpan expression while he groped for more words. "It's actually a subdivision of the Nebraska Crisis Clinic."

"Uh-huh. So you're saying Trish and Fran are actually high school age professionals?"

"Oh yeah. But part-time ones, same as me. See, sometimes these higher profile cases like yours are done undercover. You know, to protect your privacy."

Normandie carefully sipped her tea and gazed into the cup. "Well, whoever's in charge of this operation should clean that disgusting pond sometime."

"No problem. I'll be sure to tell them." He sat in a desk chair beside her. She sighed loudly, then reached over and touched his arm.

"Hey. Thanks for fishing me out, though. And uh...helping me recover in general."

"Yup. Just doing my job!"

"So you've deprogrammed a crapload of people I imagine."

"Oh sure...Some like you, but also a lot of runaway youngsters who end up in cults and stuff."

"Hmm. You definitely picked a good part of the country to do this.

I dig the mega-big sky and all. It's sort of like a warm, comforting...I don't know, nature bubble." She drank a little more tea. "Town seems nice, too. Except for that part down near the railroad tracks ..."

Dave smiled and nodded.

"I mean, there's gotta be some other nice parts of town, right?"

"There are, there are...Lots of Nebraska history in Endeavor actually, if you know where to look."

She took one more sip of orange spice and set the cup down. Moved a few inches closer to him and lay on her side. "Maybe tomorrow you can show me around a little. Hell, we can even go visit your de-programming office if you're up for that."

Dave's face scrambled for a second. He stood with his cup. "Sounds possible...Just let me know if you need anything else."

"Okay...So I really was Amanda, huh?"

"Yeah. But you're doing great now. Honest. In fact, our um, reports indicate you should be just fine to leave in another day or so." He headed for the door.

"Unless I don't want to."

Dave paused in the doorway, looked back at her. He started to say something more pointed but caught himself.

"Good night."

"Mañana..."

*   *   *

Monty Matilda zoomed east on interstate 80 in the dead of night, fresh cigar alight, frequently checking his GPS with coffeed-up eyes. His cell rang and he put it on speaker.

"About time, Delbie."

"It's three in the morning, you wanker. Where'd you go?"

"Where ya think? The Harpy won't play, so I have to seize the day—as they say. Endeavor's less than 160 kilos down the pike, mate. Straight as a billiard cue. And thanks for sleuthin' those plates."

"Right, but you could've left me a note."

"You didn't seem all that—how can I say it—enthusiastic about my plan, Delbert. Thought I'd just leave ya in your beauty sleep at the motel."

"Well I'm up now for certain. And Myra isn't gonna like this."

"Yeah? Who we workin' for, her or us? I told you. Soon as I snap a bleedin' photo archive of the little wench and nab this reward money, the Harpy's going to be wantin' to marry us."

"Well that sounds proper dreadful."

"Just an expression, mate. Back to Dreamland."

Monty tossed the phone on the seat and focused on the endless black pavement rolling under his wheels.

CHAPTER TEN:
RETURN TO MT. GARBAGE

Early the next morning, Trish and Fran jockeyed for position in front of the bathroom mirror. As usual, Fran was winning.

"Seen my eyeliner?" she asked.

"I didn't take it, Fran."

"Who's accusing?"

Trish took a deep breath, peeked into the hall. "What's Uncle Dave up to?"

"Still having his coffee. Relax."

"It's not that easy. Didn't you see him last night? Bringing in tea for her?"

"So what?"

"I bet he hasn't drank tea his entire life."

"Says who? He was around a few years before he moved in with us, y'know." Trish sighed and began manically brushing her teeth.

"Gss mbbe weeshud be muh nerfz abutem..."

"What??"

Trish nudged Fran aside to spit in the sink. "I said I guess maybe we should be more nervous about him turning her in."

"Okay. Instead of being more nervous about what?"

"What do you think?"

Fran drew another in a series of blanks.

"You don't think it's a little...creepy?"

"What, you mean Normandie and Dave??" Fran had to cough to keep from laughing. "If anything, she's just a temporary BFF—if he even knows what that means."

Trish dropped her toothbrush, went to town with her hairbrush. "I don't know..."

"Hey. Normandie is 29 years and 63 days old, and he just turned 35. So that's only like a six-year difference. Even if there was something going on, it doesn't exactly make him a peddo."

"That's not what I meant, Fran. He's our uncle. Him being all over Normandie is just...freaky."

"He made her tea, and he's taking the day off to keep tabs on her. I don't call that being all over her."

There was a familiar knock on the bathroom door.

"Time to go, girls!"

"Okay!" chirped Trish. She did a final check of herself in the mirror, then realized she had dropped some eyeliner in her shirt pocket. "Oh. This is yours." Handed it to Fran and ducked out to the hall. Fran shook her head, pocketed the eyeliner and followed.

Dave was cooking a big pot of oatmeal with their mom's embroidered apron around his waist, humming to himself. Trish stared at him as they passed through the kitchen donning their jackets and backpacks, and Fran practically had to shove her out the back door.

Five minutes later, after it was clear that Old Jeannie's battery was dead and wasn't going to turn over for at least fifteen minutes, they climbed back out of the car and started for school on foot. Trish was all sorts of annoyed, and Fran picked up on it.

"I'm not the one who left the headlights on, y'know."

"Whatever. Think you can just speed it up a little?"

"Sure, if you tell me what the rush is...What do you have first period?"

"Biology. I've been late for it three times already."

"Oh. I thought you weren't—"

Fran's phone made a horse-neighing sound, Trish's a train whistle. The alerts were simultaneous. They yanked out their devices, saw Dana's double-sent text:

MT. GARBAGE BEFORE LUNCH!

"Uh-oh," said Trish, "Ask him why."

"Already on it," said Fran.

They kept moving, hopping over a few slush puddles as they headed down the hill. Fran was an expert texter and avoided the puddles without missing one character.

"Damn. He says CAN'T TEXT RIGHT NOW."

"He just did!"

"Something smells here."

* * *

Dave sat at the kitchen table with his giant bowl of barely-touched oatmeal, leafing through the tissue-thin local newspaper for a third time. He grew impatient, tossed the paper aside and picked up the TV remote. Put on the small kitchen set and the end of a life insurance ad was followed by a ten-second teaser:

"Was Normandie Vine abducted by slave traders? Details at noon on Omaha Report—". He switched it off. Helped himself to a spoonful of oatmeal, then dropped the spoon and drummed his fingers on the table.

"What am I doing?..."

He dug into his pants pocket for a piece of paper, stared at something he'd scribbled on it the night before:

COL STATE POL 303-239-4545

He took out his cell phone, hesitated, then dialed the number. Waited.

"Yes, hi. I have some information about a missing person...Um, I'm calling from out of state. From a phone booth actually, but I can't read the number...I realize that, but yes, there's one here...There really is a phone booth here—"

"Hot damn, is that oatmeal??"

Normandie was standing at the stove behind him, her appearance as groggily frightful as ever, but with a new calmness in her eyes. She had already grabbed and filled a bowl and stood there digging in. Dave put up a "just one minute" finger and ducked away from the table.

"I'm sorry. Someone was asking me something...My name?" He lowered his voice, walked further away. "It's um, Spencer. Dave Spencer...Right...The person's name? It's um—"

"Sure is hearty and tasty, Dave-O!" She wiped a small hunk of oatmeal off her chin and flashed an achingly cute smile at him.

"You know what?" he whispered into the phone, "I um...have to be sure about something. Can I get back to you later? Thanks."

He killed the call. Took a deep breath and returned to his chair.

"Good morning!" he said. "Coffee?"

"Uh-uh. That stuff is a gateway drug."

She dropped into her chair beside him. Stretched her neck and yawned, then set her bowl down and gazed at the far wall.

"You wouldn't believe this dream I had...I was in a high school play except nobody told me about it ahead of time, and I was naked on stage when the curtain opened and I didn't know the lines, and everyone I knew was like in the first ten rows and I was having a full-blown freak-out attack so I tried to find the rope or the cord or whatever to close the curtain and the whole thing crashed on my head and knocked me over and I was suffocating and screaming but nobody was helping me—" She came back to the present and grinned. "I get that one a lot."

"Wow. Imagine you do, being in the spotlight so often..."

She pointed into her oatmeal bowl. "This is some dope gruel, y'know."

"Thanks, I guess...Added some walnuts, raisins, a little honey. Actually, it was my mom's recipe."

"Really..." She nodded, took another spoonful, then paused a long moment, whispered something nearly inaudible to herself.

"My mom died when I was eight...Roads were all slippery and she lost control of her car."

"No kidding," said Dave with a light smirk, then realized current Normandie was still using this safer version. "I mean—geez. I'm sorry. Think I might have heard about that...Or if I didn't, Trish and Fran sure did. When they were researching and all."

"Uh-huh. Those two are hard as nails, you know...Last night they told me what happened to their mom and dad."

"That so?"

"Yep. Double drug overdoses? Man, that would get anyone into deprogramming."

Dave was momentarily speechless. "Right..."

Normandie finished off her oatmeal and licked the spoon clean. "So how about I hop in the shower, and then we do what we're gonna do?"

"Okay. Which was..."

"Whatever we talked about maybe doing?"

Dave wasn't sure of his response, so Normandie didn't wait for one. She stood up, put her dirty bowl in the sink and went down the hall. A second before she disappeared into the bathroom, she pulled Trish's nightgown up over her head. Dave looked away.

* * *

At 11:57, Trish and Fran were being tortured by wall clocks. There was no second hand on these suckers, just a metallic CLICK when the minute changed. Fran was in English and making like a frog, scribbling down a homework assignment with one eye and checking the clock with the other. Trish had been watching her clock while upside down on gymnastic rings, and was now throwing her clothes back on in the locker room.

The millisecond the passing bell rang, Fran broke from class. Further texts to Dana had gone into a black hole, and as she weaved through the hordes to one of the school's side exits, her eyes scanned the hall fruitlessly for their friend's face.

Outside, a handful of smokers milled around Mt. Garbage, but Dana wasn't there yet. Trish suddenly appeared beside her, out of breath and her hair all wet.

"Where is he?"

"Got me."

They inched their way around the far side of the huge dumpster.

Dana stood at the corner of it, shaking—though more from nervousness than the cold. He saw Trish and Fran and gave them an unconvincing smile.

"Hey," said Fran, "You okay?"

He didn't answer, and Cookie Calhoun stepped around him

from the rear of the dumpster, followed by all three of the Cookie Monsters.

"Oh we're just fine, thanks."

Fran's blood boiled over. "What is this?"

"How about you tell us, Dumbwoodys? Actually—" She grabbed Heather and pulled her in front of the group. "Maybe Heather can get this power-wow going."

"It's called a pow-wow," corrected Lakota.

"Whatever." Cookie gave Heather a poke and the puniest of the Monsters took out her cell phone.

"Yeah, I saw you and Dana texting in history class the other day."

"Like that never happens?"

"Not when you're talking about someone named 'N.V.', who you might be driving back to a place called 'Peak Experience.' Who possibly is also...this person?"

She held up the selfie Dana took with Normandie in the hallway. Dana shrieked.

"Where'd you get that??" He turned to Trish and Fran, "I tried to tell you guys yesterday, remember? But you kicked me off your porch!" He looked back venomously at Heather. "Did you steal my phone, you bitch?"

"Borrowed it, dude. Just long enough to share your dorky pic." She dug back in her pocket, produced Dana's phone and tossed it back to him. Trish and Fran were beside themselves, but kept their cool.

"So she's pals with a homeless person, big deal," said Fran.

"That is no homeless person," said Heather.

"Oh yeah?" said Trish, "So who is it?"

"Oh, I think you know," said Cookie.

"All we know is you're wasting our time," said Fran. She tried to walk away but Cookie blocked her path.

"There's only one N.V. that I know from a place called Peak Experience, you dweebs. And the longer you deny it, the longer this sit-down is gonna last."

"We're standing."

Cookie sneered delightfully. If she was man enough to be

able to grow a moustache, she would have curled it. "Come on, Dumbwoodys. Admit it." She snatched Heather's phone, held up the selfie again. "Someone you know? Someone you worship?"

"Somebody you kidnapped??" barked Lakota. The Monsters menacingly surrounded Trish and Fran while keeping Dana at bay. Heather gnashed her adolescent teeth, snatched her phone back from Cookie and nearly shoved it in their faces.

"Need another look? No, don't bother. Because I know it's Normandie Vine, who I almost smashed into in the bathroom twenty seconds before Dana took—"

"WE DIDN"T KIDNAP HER!" blurted out Trish. "She tried to... steal our car."

"Oh!" cried Cookie, "So you're also harboring a criminal, in addition to the most wanted missing celebrity in America. Damn, that's greedy!" Her idiot friends chuckled in agreement.

"Tell you what, Dumbwoodys. I hear there's a sweet little reward some rich guy's offering for Normandie Vine's whereabouts—like $150,000? And there's six of us here, and I just used my phone calculator and guess what? That's 25 grand apiece. That should make for quite a few road trips to the Kearney Cornhusker Mall, don't you think?"

"Get stuffed!" said Dana, who was immediately broadsided into the snow by Cookie with a wave of her big arm. Fran stepped in.

"No one's getting a dime of that money because we're taking her back and telling them exactly what happened."

"Oh, and you think they're going to thank you? After driving her all the way to Endeavor and keeping her in your house? How about this instead? You split the $150,000 with us, and we don't turn you in today to the state police and blast your guilty kidnapping asses all over the Internet."

"Try Facebook, Twitter, Instagram, Snapchat, Periscope, Pal-Wall, Blab Feed, and Buzz Barn for starters," added Lakota.

"Well," said Fran, refusing to be rattled, "That deal sounds... possible. How about we talk to Normandie first and then meet up at the Scoop-a-Loop later to confirm—"

"I don't think so," said Cookie. "It's lunch time, isn't it? Let's cruise by your place now and have a little talk with her. Just confirming she's really there would be sort of a good start."

Fran shot her sister a brief panicked look, but it was too late. The Cookie Monsters had won. They guided them to the student parking lot while a flustered Dana stayed on his knees, digging around in the snow bank he fell into for his phone.

* * *

Ten minutes later, the Cookie Monsters roared up to Poplar Avenue in Lakota's cherry red Hyundai, Trish and Fran stuffed into the back seat on both sides of Cookie.

"Stay here," she said to Lakota and Heather in front, "This won't take long."

"You mean we don't get to meet her?" whined Lakota.

"You'll get your turn if you shut up." She climbed out with Trish and Fran, and followed them to the front door. Fran nudged Trish as they neared the steps.

"Dave's car is gone," she whispered.

"I know..." Trish whispered back.

Trish unlocked the door and they stepped into the front hall.

"Hello??" She waited all of four seconds for a response. "Oh well, looks like she left."

"Hang on," said Cookie, peering into every front room and down the hallway. "Where'd she go?"

"Probably halfway back to Colorado by now," said Fran, "I mean, our uncle took the day off to hang with her, and he's not here either, so he must've talked her into taking her back. Too bad. We'll miss her—"

"Wait a damn minute. Call him and find out."

"Sorry, we can't do that. He never answers his phone. Barely knows how to use one, right Trish?"

"Yeah, he's the worst!"

Cookie studied their faces with her poisonous eyes. "Okay, losers. But I swear. If you're lying, you're gonna regret the day your dead momma spit you out." She started back to the Hyundai. Trish and Fran looked at each other, then whispered again simultaneously.

"Where'd they go?"   "I don't know."

* * *

Across town, Dave drove Normandie around a treeless, nondescript neighborhood of nondescript ranch homes. Normandie wore Trish's pink Hello Kitty stocking cap, a new pair of cheap drug store sunglasses, and looked completely bored. Dave wasn't.

"The advantage of this neighborhood, see, is you don't need to do any leaf raking. Would certainly suggest it to anyone if there were some real garages instead of these useless carports, though."

"Damn. If I bought a house on this street it would have to come with another pond." He glanced at her with alarm and she grinned, nudged him. "Just a joke, Dave-o!"

He half-smiled, and then his cell phone rang. Fumbled with the wheel and Normandie grabbed it and steered while he took out the phone.

"Thanks—Hello?...Oh hi Patty...What's that again?..." He took the wheel back, thanked Normandie again with a nod. "No kidding... Did you try re-booting it?..Uh-huh...Well, it isn't the best time, but I suppose I could swing by...Okay." He hung up, braked the Volvo and began to wheel it around.

"Got some programming problems at the old de-programming office?" asked Normandie.

"Right. This won't take long." He made a left and headed back to the main road. "Actually, this is happening at my veterinarian cover job."

"You mean a pet doc? Pret-ty craf-ty!"

Ten minutes later, Dave warily entered the clinic reception room. It was thankfully empty, and he turned to hold the door open for Normandie. She glanced around at a few heartwarming dog and cat posters and beamed.

"Wow. Sweet cover."

"Yeah, it can be pretty comforting work sometimes. Especially between stressful de-programming cases. Now let's see if—"

He jumped a little as Patty entered from the hall carrying a plastic water jug.

"Oh, hi Doctor!" She saw Normandie standing there in her bizarre outfit and her cheery expression dissolved. The disguise was working.

"Hi Patty, this is, um..."

"Amanda hi," blurted out Normandie with a little smile and wave.

"Our guest from out-of-town," continued Dave.

"Oh..." muttered Patty, and turned to water a sad plant behind the reception desk with the jug.

"Still can't log in?" asked Dave.

"Nope."

"And you tried re-booting?"

"Yup."

"O-kay! Well I better have a look then." He started for the hall and Normandie quickly tapped his shoulder.

"Hey. Mind if I visit your pets while you do your IT thing?"

"We don't like people doing that," snapped Patty, "Most of them are under special care, and we're not—"

"This one time it's fine," said Dave. "Amanda's sort of um...family."

Patty used every facial muscle she had to dredge up a smile.

A dozen or so cages lined both sides of a short hall. There were a couple of fight-injured cats, a rabbit with a bandaged ear, a guinea pig with a tiny cone on its head, and a shaking Chihuahua/Jack Russell mix named Heinrich with one of its paws in a cast. Normandie stopped at this one and read the index card slotted into the door.

"Aww. Poor Heinie..." She opened the cage without hesitating and reached inside to pet the dog. "Who's your friend, baby?...That's right..."

Dave had opened the door to a small server room and was beside himself trying to figure out how to get the office computers working again. The cheat sheet he had in his hand certainly wasn't helping. He pushed a few buttons, typed in a login and password for maybe the fifth time. Panel lights that were supposed to be green blinked red. He groaned loudly as Normandie appeared behind him, Heinrich cradled in her arms.

"How's it going?"

"Don't ask..."

"Too late!" He turned with some annoyance and saw her holding the dog.

"Oh no. You can't be doing that, Normandie."

"Doing what?"

"Taking our patients out of their cages!"

"I thought you told Tammy it was fine."

"Her name is Patty, and no, it's not fine."

"Look at him, though! He's not shaking anymore!"

Dave was ready to tear his hair out, but instead jabbed in the login and password again. "Just let me get this stinkin' server going, and I'll put him back for you..."

"A server? I take it you checked all the juice vessels."

"The what?"

"Hold Heinie a second." She handed him the dog, wheeled the server's cart around to the side and made sure every connecting cord was in tight. "Okay, rock 'n' roll..." He sat there with a muddled expression. "Try it again!"

He handed her the dog back, logged in again, hit RETURN and the green lights came on like a Christmas tree.

"Cool," she said, and started for the hall with Heinie. "Where to next?"

* * *

Meg Strump was passed out drunk on her living room sofa when Monty Matilda's van rolled up and parked across the street from the Dunwoody house. Monty recognized the Ford Focus in the driveway immediately, then its license plate, and chuckled gleefully. He killed the engine and climbed out with his camera. Snapped away at the

Focus, the house and the street so rapidly he didn't even look in the viewfinder.

The Dunwoodys had an old-fashioned flag mailbox on the curb. It was a hand-carved and stained wooden barn, no doubt made by some local craftsperson or bought at a flea market, but that didn't matter to Monty. It was a mailbox.

He looked around for a possible witness, then crossed the street, opened the thing, and plucked out two utility bills. Both were addressed to DAVID T. DUNWOODY.

Minutes later, he was sitting in the van again and on his phone. Delbert grumbled a hello.

"Top o' the plaza, mate! Get y'self a pen."

"For what now?"

"For the name of the poor bastard who could be up on Vine-napping charges today if you shake your bunghole and do what I tell ya. David Dunwoody, 12 Poplar Lane, Endeavor, Knee-braska. 68869. Get me everything you can find on him."

There was a pause on the line. "I don't know, Monty."

"You don't know what?"

"If I can get what you're asking for."

"Why the bloody not?"

"Well...Have to say being your photo caddy hasn't been all that cost-effecting for me...Understand?"

Monty's face turned redder and ruddier by the second.

"I mean, we're flyin' everywhere, I can't sleep, I eat weird food which gives me the squelches once a week and I never even get a photo credit."

"Maybe that's because you don't take the photos, you ungrateful pup. If it wasn't for me bailin' out your drunk arse in Brisbane that night you'd still be losin' wages in all-night snooker dens."

"Yeah, well I got ideas for a better future in front of me now, and this piddle work don't figure in."

"You'd really do this to me today, Delbert? Right when we're on the brink of a big bloomin' payoff?"

"Yeah, Monty. I would. And I am."

"C'mon, Delbie. One more time. Just put on your lapper, type in David Dunwoody. It's easy."

"Bleedin' right it is. So do it yourself."

CLICK.

"Delbie?...DELBERT?"

He mouthed something that was even unprintable in Australia. Dropped the phone on the seat and drove away.

CHAPTER ELEVEN:
FOUR OR FIVE TIMES

Fran sat at a long table in the school library, pretending to study from her propped-up history book while texting Trish inside it:
Fran: HE WAS MAKING OATMEAL, NOT WRITING A POEM. RELAX ALREADY.
Trish: THEN WHERE DID THEY GO?
Fran: IDK TIMES TWO. SHE'S BEEN WEARING YOUR CLOTHES SINCE SHE GOT HERE. MAYBE HE TOOK HER TO WALMART.
Trish: YOU THINK THAT'S OKAY? HER OUT IN PUBLIC?
Fran: PROB STILL DISGUISED. & YOU BEING STRESSY ISN'T HELPING.

Mrs. Appleworth the school librarian strolled by, flicking a very sharp pencil in her hand. Fran shut her book a moment and pretended to write a note. When she went back to her phone, Trish had already texted her back:
Trish: HEARD FROM DANA?
Fran: NOPE. PROB TOO BUSY HAVING HIS OWN BREAKDOWN.
A balled-up sticky note smacked her in the face. Fran looked up at Trish, who had been texting her from directly across the long table. I'M NOT BREAKING DOWN she wrote.
Fran: FOOLED ME.
Trish: WHAT DO WE DO ABOUT THE COOKIE MONSTERS? THEY'LL BE WATCHING THE HOUSE.
Fran: EASY. JUST SHINE A LIGHT ON 'EM.
Trish: HUH?? YOU MEAN 'SHINE 'EM ON'?
Fran: YEAH, WHATEV. LET'S ENJOY OUR LAST NIGHT WITH N.V., THEN TALK DAVE INTO DRIVING HER BACK WITH US FIRST THING.

Trish sighed, then gave Fran a resigned nod across the table.

* * *

Mt. Loup was actually little more than a high bluff, rising 790 feet out of a field of shivering prairie grass about three miles northeast of town. The trail leading to its summit passed through a small grove of cottonwoods, some still sporting yellow leaves, and Dave led Normandie up the path and over some slippery rocks and roots. They were both winded, and Normandie's cheeks were as red as cherry cider.

"You didn't tell me this was going to be torture," she said.

"Aw, c'mon. Weren't you just in the Rocky Mountains?"

"That's different. I was whacked out."

"Yeah, I know...Have to say I like you a lot better this way. And you were pretty damn good with Heinie at the clinic."

"Well...had some pet turtles when I was a kid, but that was about it. They died like every three weeks...But I really did think about becoming a vet myself once. Before I got sidetracked with this singing thing."

Dave chuckled, as they rounded a sharp curve and broke out of the trees at the top. There was a rusted-out iron guardrail, and a sweeping view of Endeavor and dozens of prairie miles.

"Check it out!"

Normandie took a step toward the rail, then recoiled. "Can I check it from here?"

"Oh. Scared of heights?"

"You could say that."

"Too bad. When it's super clear you can see about 40 miles in every direction. A few times I've come up here at night to dig on the stars. Sometimes meteor showers."

"Stars are kind of a no-show in L.A. Can you see the Rockies from here?"

"Naw, that's a little far." He pointed to the west. "They'd be in that direction, though."

Normandie gathered herself and inched a bit closer to the rail. Dave stepped aside to give her room, then circled around behind her and Normandie let out a shriek. Jumped back.

"I'm sorry!" she cried, "I don't know why I did that!"

"You okay?"

"No..." She clenched a fist and pounded the rail with it. "GOD I miss Sofia so much!"

"Sofia?"

"Never mind...Can we just go back down?"

Dave nodded, started back down the path over some rocks. Turned and instinctively put out his hand. She hesitated, but took it.

Minutes later, they exited the trail to a patch of frozen dirt where they had parked the Volvo. Normandie had her hands stuffed back in her coat pocket and they weren't talking, but when she got in the passenger seat and Dave started the car to warm it up, she reached down between the seats and slid out his CD of old country swing.

"This looks cool. Think I'd like it?"

"Um...you might. Far as I know, it's pretty different from the stuff you do."

She shrugged. "Then that could be a good thing, right?" She plucked the CD out of its case and handed it to him. "Crank up this bad boy."

He popped it into the player. Milton Brown and His Musical Brownies doing "Four or Five Times" came on. Normandie giggled, and her foot was tapping on the Volvo floor within seconds.

"This rocks! I mean—swings!"

Dave smiled from ear to ear. She danced her fingers on her pants leg, then up his sleeve like a marionette and gave him a fetching smile.

"Know how to work stuff?"

"Work?"

"Yeah, you know. Dance!"

"Um, yeah. A little."

She threw her door open. "You're on, Dave-o!"

Dave sat there a frozen moment, then got out. Reached back in to goose the volume. Normandie went around to his side of the car, and held out her hand as ladylike as she could manage. He took the lead, and within seconds they were country-swing dancing in the frozen mud.

* * *

Monty Matilda had spent a good twenty minutes digging through databases in search of information on David T. Dunwoody, but was too impatient to look for a place in town with actual wi-fi, so had to settle for using his phone on the side of the road. Bad enough he was forced to do the grunt work that rat of a former colleague Delbert handled; now he needed to control himself while his fat, sweaty thumbs made frequent spelling mistakes on the tiny keyboard.

Once he finally learned the make and model of Dave's Volvo, he shook the van back to life and covered every inch of Endeavor at least twice for close to an hour, more frustrated by the second. He made a wrong turn at a T-juncture at one point and found himself on a two-lane road out of town that he didn't realize was wrong until he passed a boarded-up produce stand he didn't remember, stomped his brake and nearly slid into a ditch. After a full half-minute of unintelligible blue cursing, he fished the last beer out of a water-filled cooler and glugged half of it down. Peered ahead down the unfamiliar road and spotted a nearby bluff rising out of some trees.

Dave's CD player was now on its third song, "The Tennessee Waltz", and he was actually doing one with Normandie. They were shivering slightly but their hearts were warm, and while Normandie hummed along with her eyes closed, letting her partner lead her, Dave tried in vain to keep himself from grinning—or crying.

The years he had spent trying to amend for that fateful, stupid night with his roadie friends—raising Trish and Fran, throwing himself into veterinary science, even keeping his hair short—only masked a pain he hadn't realized until this very moment: He missed his brother and sister-in-law so, so much.

Meanwhile, neither Dave nor Normandie noticed the van that had rolled to a stop across from the dirt road, maybe a football field away. And the large man with the giant telephoto lens leaning out its window.

* * *

A few hours later, Myra was having lunch with Howard at her favorite corner table at Le Estomac in Beverly Hills. Myra had returned to town after getting a few more phone messages from entertainment channels requesting interviews, because those things were always easier to schedule from her home turf, and there was an office she had to make sure wasn't slacking off in her absence.

She enjoyed the first good sleep she'd had in days in her Brentwood apartment, even without a sleeping mask, and was happy to be back holding court in her favorite eatery. Two Warner Bros. executives had already given her hugs on her way in, and she and Howard had ordered their food within moments of sitting down. Myra preferred that because it gave her extra phone time.

"No. Can't do 3:00," she was saying to someone, "We're giving Matt Lauer another chance then and I hear he's going to cry. How's 5:30?"

Howard looked over, shook his head and mouthed the word CONAN.

"Never mind. Skip 5:30. And you know what, Ellen? This is taking too long. Get back to me with three other times and we'll go from there."

She dropped her phone on the perfectly pressed pink tablecloth and looked at Howard. "It is so hard to raise media lapdogs... Anything new from Colorado?"

"Er—no. Two hundred more man-hours, twenty more German Shepherds, couple of helicopters."

"Sounds perfect." She suddenly grimaced and flagged down a passing waiter. "Excuse me. I ordered the Chilled Caesar Salad, not one from the Arctic Circle." The waiter nodded and took her plate away. Howard glanced around, then leaned in a lot closer than he normally did.

"Myra? Where do you think Normandie actually is?"

She gave it maybe three seconds of thought. "Hibernating. It's not like she hasn't done this before. Weren't you with us that time in Seattle? Found her a week later, shacked up in some Tibetan acupuncturist's hovel in the Cascades."

"Yeah, but...Aren't you worried about her?"

"Sure I am, Howard. Like I would be about a Palm Beach condo during hurricane season. The difference being the condo doesn't need me."

A handsome, prematurely grey man wearing jeans and a European-cut sports jacket appeared at the table.

"Hello Myra, great to see you."

"Hi Garth, so great to see you too." She let him take her hand and squeeze it.

"So...any word?"

She sighed and shook her head morosely. Instinctively picked up her table napkin as if about to use it on her eyes. "Afraid not."

"We're all thinking of you."

"Thanks, Garth. Say hello to your family."

"I'll do that."

Myra waited for him to leave, then dropped the napkin again. "Poor son-of-a-bitch hasn't made a watchable movie since you were in knee socks." Her phone vibrated once and she grabbed it. "Who's this now?" She looked at the front, then handed it to Howard. "Or should I say *what's* this?"

Howard stared at a texted photo of something written on a sheet of paper, and taken inside a vehicle. "Looks like a bunch of numbers."

"I'm up to speed with you there, Howard. What the hell are they??"

The phone suddenly vibrated in his hand.

"Oh! Monty Matilda!"

"Shit..."

She snatched it back and answered.

"Whatever that was, I probably don't want to know."

"Did you write those delicious digits down?"

"If I wanted to call you for a date, Monty, I wouldn't have deleted your number four years ago."

"Very high-sterical. And also missing the point by an outback kilometer. Those would be the numbers of my newest direct deposit banking account, luv, where I trust you will put two hundred and fifty thousand American dollars in the next 24 hours."

"And I should do something completely batshit like this...why?"

Monty sat with his phone and a "Nebraska Cold Brew" at a tiny table in the Lonesome Drip, surrounded by no one except Butchie, who had run over from the hardware store to fire up the Keurig for his lone customer in between staple gun sales. Monty had his camera with him, and was scrolling through dozens of recent Dave and Normandie shots.

"Because I'm currently feasting on a series of photographs—and one very entertaining 30-second video—of your missing golden child dancing with a strange fellah in a godforsaken cowboy country parking lot."

"Where is that exactly, Monty?"

"Now I realize I can splash this prize package around the world to every tabloid contact and claim that $150,000 reward payment today, or I can take one hundred grand more from Harp Worldwide Management and keep my big ruddy lips closed for say...another week?"

"You miserable slice of excrement."

"Thank you. And I'll take that as a pass. Enjoy cleaning up the mess, luv—"

"WAIT!"

Myra motioned for Howard to stand up and pay the bill. "We might have a deal, Monty. Okay? But I'm in a Gelson's checkout line right now. Let me call a few people and I'll get right back to you." She hung up without waiting for his answer, then ushered Howard to the exit.

"Call that tech geek we use, whatever his name is. Murphy? O'Reilly? Fitzpatrick?"

"You mean Gonzalez?"

"Right, him. Give him Monty's cell number and see if he can trace it."

"I think we had to keep Monty on the line for that—"

"I don't care! Call him!"

Howard slipped a parking ticket to the valet as they reached the curb and got on his phone. It rang before he could even dial a number.

"Harp Worldwide, this is Howard."

"Hey yeah," said a somewhat familiar and possibly hungover male voice, "Who do I call to get that Normandie Vine reward money?"

"Well...certainly not me, sir. I think there was a num—"

"This is Delbert Smith by the way. Y'know, Monty Matilda's work slave?"

Howard whirled and shot Myra a look of disbelief. Stepped away for more privacy.

"Or maybe I should say ex-work slave—"

"Yes Delbert, I know who you are. Tell me: Are you with Monty right now?"

"Shit, no. I sacked his sorry widebottom ass when he left me here and went to Endeavor."

"Endeavor? What is that? Another retreat?"

"Naw, just some Nebraska dirt clod town where she's holed up with this family. Dangwoodies or Dungwoody, somethin' like that. Wanted me to dig into the guy and I said no flippin' way, I'm not your research lackey, I wanna get PAID—"

"Okay Delbert. Listen." He flashed an elated thumbs-up to an anxious Myra as the valet pulled her Mercedes up to the curb. "I'm in touch with the people who work the reward hotline, so I will pass along your number right away, and someone will get back to you soon. Do you understand?"

He hung up, danced a mini-jig on the sidewalk and hopped into Myra's passenger seat beside her. "You can say anything you want to me, Myra. But don't ever say I don't earn my salary."

"Don't get all peacocky. Where is she?"

He went back on his phone. "Endeavor, Nebraska. Probably nothing but a gas station and a McDonald's, but I'll hit up Google Maps right now and find out."

"Damn. We have to move on this."

"That's what I'm doing!"

"No, not that. I don't care if she's in a trailer park by the Salton Sea. We have to cash this thing in before anyone else does. Cancel everyone I booked and get Paul Stein on the phone."

"You mean Paul Stein the showrunner?"

"No, I mean Gertrude the artist. Yes, Howard. Paul Stein!"

CHAPTER TWELVE:
MAYNARD'S HORSES

Normandie and the Dunwoodys finished their dinner in near silence. Trish and Fran were scheduled to make spaghetti and meatballs on their own that night but they were both a little unnerved about Dave taking Normandie out to "show her the town" and "do some errands". It wasn't so much creepiness about any kind of age difference—which again, wasn't that far apart—but the fact that any precious time they still had with Normandie was dwindling.

While Fran was hibernating in her room listening to speed grunge on her earbuds, Dave and Normandie had stayed in the kitchen, making the meatballs and sauce while Trish boiled the pasta and warily watched them collaborate. Now, as Trish sat and observed their guest twirl as much spaghetti as possible onto her fork, with Fran barely touching her own food or even looking up from her plate, action needed to be taken.

"Hey Normandie!" said Trish, "Can I show you my Web site after dinner?"

Fran sank even lower in her chair, but Normandie perked up. "Sure damn can! What's on it?"

"Oh...personal music stuff. I sing, write songs sometimes. When I'm not in school and helping deprogram. Got a whole bunch of followers even."

"She does have a nice voice," added Dave.

"Thought you had a lot of homework tonight," said Fran.

"Oh, I'll get it done," returned Trish, cuttingly.

"Hell, I'm done," said Normandie, and glanced at Dave, "Okay if we hit the Internet now? With NO celebrity sites, I promise."

Dave shrugged. Since she had asked him to dance out at Mt. Loup, he had basically become a dutiful puppy dog. "Be my guest!"

"Too late, already am!" Normandie got up with her plate, grabbed Trish's and took them to the sink. Even Fran seemed almost impressed by that. The moment they went down the hall, though, she turned to her uncle.

"She burned a few of the meatballs, you know."

"C'mon, that wasn't a big deal. It was her first time making them. Or practically anything, from what I could tell."

Awkward silence flooded back in as they polished off their dinners.

"Oh yeah," said Dave, "Don't forget to feed Maynard's horses after dinner. He has his physical therapy tonight."

"I know, I know…" She tried a final bite of food, but made a face and let it fall off her fork. "So what kind of errands were you guys doing all day."

"Nothing special. Had to pick up some extra gauze for the clinic. Normandie stayed in the car for that stop."

"You left her in the car??"

"She wasn't going anywhere, Fran. She likes it here, remember?"

"Right…So all you did for hours was get gauze?"

"And we stopped at the clinic and she met Patty—in disguise, of course. And then drove around town a bit."

He drank some ice water. Fran eyed him. "Think I'm done too." She stood up.

"Hey. Do you know who Sofia is?" Fran thought for a moment and shook her head, took her plate to the sink. "That's strange," said Dave, "because she said she missed her at one point today. But wouldn't elaborate."

Normandie lay on Trish's bed while the PC booted up.

"I bet I've exhausted your whole wardrobe by now."

"Just about. There might be a nightshirt or two you haven't tried…"

Normandie grinned, then rolled over and peered down for a second. "Hey, what's with all these posters of me you keep under the bed?"

"Huh? Oh right! Research materials!"

Normandie looked puzzled.

"Basically," continued Trish, "When we're assigned a de-programming subject we're given all sorts of materials on them to study. Those DVDs you saw in the den were part of that. Which...you also weren't supposed to find...Okay, check it out!"

Normandie rose and went behind Trish's desk chair. Her site was called TRISH DUNWOODY GETS VOCAL, simply designed in pink and sky blue with a few badly animated "singing flowers". She clicked on a video link. Trish appeared on a small, dimly-lit stage clutching a microphone, singing Cindi Lauper's "Time After Time" with the lyrics scrolling up a screen beside her.

"This was a year or so ago. At Cary's Okie Lounge over in Grand Island."

"Awesome," said Normandie politely.

"You can't see them on camera but there were almost fifteen people there listening to me."

Her voice cracked a few times, but the rendition was pleasant enough. Normandie smiled and was about to retreat to the bed. Trish quickly hit a drop-down to a bookmark and a YouTube video came up. Trish in her backyard, summertime, seated with an acoustic guitar—and actually playing it rather well.

"Did this one on Periscope and transferred it over. You ever scope?"

"Not much. Though I suppose I should..." She returned to the desk, crouched and cocked her head slightly. "I think I know this one."

"It's 'The Fear' by a British singer, Lily Allen?"

"Right..."

Trish gave Normandie her chair, and Video Trish began to sing. Her voice had smoothed, sweetened. It was rich with feeling and Normandie let it transport her.

I want to be rich and I want lots of money
I don't care about clever I don't care about funny
I want loads of clothes and craploads of diamonds
I heard people die while they are trying to find them

"You do a real good version of that, Trish," said Normandie.

Trish beamed brighter than the sun. "You really like it? Wow... Anyway, you definitely need to use Periscope. Real easy way to market yourself. I've been thinking of doing a morning Scope, and a night Scope, and an afternoon—"

Fran suddenly walked in the room, pulling on her jacket.

"Anybody wanna feed Maynard's horses with me?"

Trish made a sour face, not keen on having her moment with Normandie interrupted. "Nope," she said, without turning around.

"You guys deprogram horses too?"

"Naw, just helping out a neighbor. Wanna come?"

Normandie was afraid to answer, sensing Trish's sour vibe.

"Go ahead," Trish muttered. "You can watch this anytime."

"You sure?" Normandie asked.

"Whatever. I'm hittin' it," said Fran, and marched back out.

Maynard Mellon was in his 70s and lived about a half mile up Juniper Road, which was all dirt and branded with tractor tire marks. He'd hit a rock in his field a few months back with his John Deere, tumbled out, broken a few vertebrae, and now needed occasional help with Buster and Duster, his old mares and best friends.

Fran got only two yards up the road from Poplar when Normandie raced up behind her, already out of breath. In the distance, Fran could see Trish standing at the corner waiting for them to hook up before vanishing back in the house.

"I love horses," said Normandie, "Pretty rockin' that Dave also works as a vet by the way."

"Oh. Yeah."

A little ways up the rutted road, a large barn approached in the three-quarter moonlight. Normandie wrapped the sweatshirt she got from Trish a bit tighter. "I do wanna Google your deprogramming group when I get a chance. Maybe on Trish's computer later. Or actually...maybe there's a place around here I can pick up a new smart phone tomorrow. Starting to jones for tweets."

"We'll have to see, okay? I mean—I should talk to my colleagues about that. A big part of the deprogramming process is staying off line."

Normandie gave her a decided frown as they reached the barn. Fran unlatched and swung open its big door. She switched on a dim overhead light and two horses in adjacent stalls shook themselves awake.

"Meet Buster and Duster!" announced Fran. Normandie cooed, went up and stroked each of their noses and cooed some more.

"I don't know which is which, but I don't care," she said.

"Duster's the grey one, Buster the black one. I've ridden them a few times. Duster's the girl but she's faster."

"That's appropriate."

Fran giggled a little, feeling more like herself around Normandie. She reached into the stable for the horses' two water bowls, walked them over to a hose and dumped out what was in there. Began refilling them. Normandie kept on alternating her nose petting, and Fran turned to watch her. In the muted barn light, without any makeup and days removed from affect, she looked pretty angelic.

"What do they eat?"

"Chopped oat straw. There's a 12-pound bag of the stuff over there."

She pointed to a nearby corner. Normandie walked over, got the bag, brought it back, and began tossing some into each stable. Fran put the filled water bowls back in, then helped Normandie with the oat straw. The horses went to town on it. Fran took a couple of carrots out of her pocket, handed one to Normandie and they let the horses eat them out of their hands. The girls chuckled, knocked some of the straw off their clothes. Fran kept on fidgeting, obviously nervous.

"Hey Normandie?"

"Yeah..."

"I um, just wanted to say how much it means to me that you're here. As a deprogramming subject, I mean."

"Thanks...I guess me flipping out and all was kind of a blessing for both of us."

"Sure was."

They continued to stand and watch the horses feed. Fran sensed an odd tension between them, a kind she had some trouble identifying.

"Pretty amazing I was Amanda Mushnik again for a little while..."

"Sure were..."

"I mean, I know it's hard to believe, but Amanda was really a hot little mess."

Fran smiled. Worked up some courage and gave her a nudge on the elbow.

"Hey...Was this 'Aunt Sophie' in Arcadia you once stayed with actually named Sofia?"

Normandie's face twitched noticeably. She stared down at the hay on the floor, and flipped some of it into the air with her shoe. "Only the best nanny of all time. Ever hear of Gloria Estefan?"

"I think so. Didn't Madonna play her in a movie?"

"No, that was Evita someone. Gloria was Cuban-American with the Miami Sound Machine, and Sofia played and sang her stuff all day and night, and it inspired the crap out of me. For a long time kids made fun of me in school, until I started singing in the cafeteria in sixth grade."

"That's awesome...You still talk to her? Sofia, I mean..."

Normandie's expression darkened. "Nope. You got another carrot?"

Fran fished one out, handed it to her. "Y'know, Normandie, when I was in sixth grade—years before I started taking advanced psychology classes, of course—I used to get bullied a lot myself."

"That sucks. How come?"

Fran shrugged. "No good reason. Bunch of us were on a sleepover at a friend's house and watched *An Officer and a Gentleman*. Every one of my girl friends had a crush on Richard Gere, but I was all over Debra Winger. Had been since she rode that fake bull in *Urban Cowboy*, and I think I said as much.

"Anyway, it got around school eventually and kids started calling me Winger-Zinger and Bush Pilot and I can't tell you what else. I was in the dumps big time." She paused to sink down and take a seat on the hay-strewn floor. "Meadow Road goes right over the interstate a few miles from here, so I rode my bike down there one day." Her voice deflated like a child's balloon. "And I almost jumped off the bridge."

Normandie hesitated, then reached down and put a warm hand on Fran's shoulder. Fran stiffened a moment, before quickly grabbing Normandie's hand and holding it for dear life.

"Believe me..." she continued, "If there were drugs around in 6th grade, or if I knew what the hell they were, I would've been using them. Instead...I heard you do 'Toaster in My Heart' that night on the radio...and it perked me up—"

"Wow. I never even liked that song. But hey—I'm glad *you* did."

Fran let go of Normandie's hand a moment to erase a tear from her eye, then grabbed it back again. Beside them, Duster offered a friendly neigh. Normandie patted his nose with her free hand.

"It's okay baby," she said, "Normie's here." Normandie was speaking to the horse, but deep down, the words were meant for Fran. And Fran knew it.

* * *

When they got back to the house, Fran said good night and went in her room. Trish was still on the computer, scrolling through emails. Normandie looked in on Dave, who was on his bed reading the *People* magazine with her on the cover. He quickly flipped it over and set it aside as she entered.

"Hey there. How'd the horses go?"

"Fine..." Her voice and gaze trailed off.

"You okay?"

She nodded, turned and softly closed the door after her. Dave was suddenly a bit nervous.

"I think I want to go back tomorrow."

He took a long second to react. "Oh. O-kay. Did something—"

"No, no. Just starting to believe that I mean more to a lot of my fans than I thought I did. So...I may as well just face the music again.

In more ways than one."

"Well...Suppose we'll head out first thing in the a.m. then. I'll tell the girls—"

"Actually, don't. Just text them from the road or something. It might be a little too much for them to hear."

"Sure...Yeah...But aren't you going to sleep in one of their rooms again?"

"I don't think so. I'll find somewhere new." She paused until Dave's face flushed slightly, then winked at him. "That big couch in the den's got me written all over it, Dave-o."

He looked momentarily disappointed, then worked up a relieved smile. "Right. Help yourself!'

* * *

An hour later, the Cookie Monsters were in Lakota's basement rec room, surrounded by hair band posters and empty beer cans. Lakota woozily took out her cell phone.

"Okay, Cook. Give it."

Cookie paused for dramatic effect, then looked at a note she'd put on her own phone.

"1. 800." Lakota began dialing on hers. "371-3946."

The others waited breathlessly. Lakota frowned.

"It's transferring somewhere...To a different number!"

"Should we write it down?"

"No wait. It's a recording...Okay...+39...zero...uhh, and eight more numbers."

"What's '+39' mean?" asked Heather, cracking open another beer.

"Oh shit!" yelled Lakota, and quickly hung up. "Forget it. We can't do this."

"Excuse me?" sneered Cookie. "We are not passing up reward money, Lakota. Did you dial the same number they had on TV—"

"Yeah! But they were gonna charge me for a second one and my parents would've killed me."

"For what??"

"For the stupid number being in Italy!"

* * *

Two hours after that, Monty stretched out on the fully-reclined passenger seat of his van. He was parked at the far end of Poplar Avenue. Frigid November air tried to fight its way inside, and he calmly used a bottle of cheap malt liquor to put himself to sleep.

He raised his phone, checked its messages and emails for what must have been the tenth time in the last hour. Then he dialed Myra Harp's number and waited to hear the recording of her nasal bark and subsequent beep.

"Myra? Monty again...Your work-husband...Still waitin' for you to confirm our deal...It's really the only way, Myra...Delbert's become a ripe pissant and all the better now, 'cause that's more green stuff for us, right? Anyway luv, I'll be nice and give ya till ten in the mornin', that's noon my country bumpkin time...Can't wait to hear your lovely voice..."

He hung up and was dozing with the phone in his hand in seconds.

* * *

At 3:30 in the morning, Dana was still sitting at his Mac with all the lights off and plummeting deep into Photoshop. The lone selfie he took with Normandie at the high school exit had become an art project. Six different versions of the shot filled the screen, as he experimented with sepia tones, an iris effect, color and hue saturations—even a "wet" filter that made them look like they were submerged underwater.

Dana's eyes were glazed over from a combination of sleep deprivation and enchantment, and he let the mouse guide his hand like a Ouija board planchette.

"So which one do you like, Normandie?...I'm kind of hot on the sepia version. Seriously vintage, right?" Dana paused to listen to the thin air beside him, then chuckled devilishly.

CHAPTER THIRTEEN: AT 700 HOURS

Butchie was scrubbing out the inside of the Lonesome Drip's Keurig machine at dawn when a rented Lincoln town car and two navy vans from Omaha A/V Rentals bounced over the train tracks, roared through Endeavor and up the hill.

"Dang!" he muttered to himself, "Least they ain't ambulances..." The vehicles were still puzzling enough to force him out to the sidewalk and futilely peer around Main Street in search of another local soul he could discuss them with.

Up on Poplar Avenue, the Beansmith's Dark Roast was already brewing on its automatic timer. Dave was showered, dressed and brushing his teeth. Normandie was awake for a change and nearly ready, seated on the sheeted living room couch and wearing the last of Trish's borrowed sweats available, her hair a typical sleepy fright. She rose, stretched, and sauntered down the hall to Dave's door. Lightly knocked.

"All set, Dave-O?"

"Just about."

She stood there a moment, then turned to take in Trish and Fran's closed doors. Let out a little sigh and whispered to herself.

"See ya, womenz...Thanks for the bitchin' deprogramming."

The toilet flushed in Dave's bathroom. Seconds later, the doorbell rang. Dave didn't hear it.

"Should I get that?"

He didn't hear her either, so Normandie shrugged and went to the door.

Opened it a crack and Chuck, Rashid, Myra Harp, and a 50ish man with tanning booth skin and a wool sweater tied over his dress shirt and slacks bulldozed into the house. Normandie gave a little yelp, backpedaled, and fell over an umbrella stand by the door. Myra rushed up and caressed her cheek with a thin, cold hand.

"My sweet angel. I was so worried about you..."

Chuck and Rashid were already busy casing the house like secret service men when Dave came down the hall, utter shock on his face.

"Excuse me—"

"Paul Stein, Chaos Theory Productions." His tanned hand was already out, and Dave was so blinded by the man's white teeth he shook it in a state of near paralysis.

"Who the hell are—"

"We do reality projects you've probably heard of. *Babysitter Challenge? Delinquent Island? Just Try to Not Eat That?* All very well-received."

"Nobody watches those things here—"

"In Nebraska? Oh, but they certainly do."

"I mean in this house—"

"Even better then! This one should be much more natural."

Dave squinted at the two of them. "What do you mean this one?"

"Oh my God! Myra Harp!!"

It was Trish, standing in the kitchen beside an equally shell-shocked Fran. Myra strode up wearing her full plastic grin and quickly shook their hands before they were any more awake.

"A pleasure. Monty Matilda thought you might be terror-extortionists or something but I was so relieved to learn you were nothing but big Normandie fans. Here girls, add these to your collection..." She reached into a large tote bag and handed them two vintage "Euro Vine Tour" concert posters.

Normandie gaped at Trish and Fran a long moment, then slowly got to her feet, her face a shape-shifting mask of sheer disgust.

"You mean ...you guys are not actual deprogrammers? I frickin' trusted you!"

"Actual de-WHAT?" asked an incredulous Myra.

"No Normandie," said Dave in a rush, "But we can explain what happened—"

"Not now, pops," said Myra. "First we discuss business. Paul?"

Stein bent his knees slightly and threw out his hands, as if about to launch into a Broadway show tune. "*Thanksgiving with Normandie. Think of it as a coming-out-of-rehab party. Wanting to do nothing but get clean and sober and win back her reputation as America's pop sweetheart, Normandie Vine lands in a small Nebraska town for a holiday dinner with an average Midwest family.*"

"What?? There's nothing average about us!" cried Fran, "We lost our damn parents ten years ago. Dave's our uncle and he operates on parakeets for a living." Normandie's mouth dropped open even wider.

"Even better!" cried Stein, "A family striving to heal itself by taking in this wayward, troubled star. There won't be a dry seat in the house."

"Think of the numbers we'll pull," added Myra, "Oooh! My chills are getting chills." Normandie turned and left the room, Rashid following.

"I can't believe this," continued Fran, "You want to turn her into a stupid reality star?"

"It's helped a few people, hasn't it?" said Myra.

"It's a JOKE!"

Trish ran up to Dave. "Normandie's a talented musician and actress. You can't let this happen, Uncle Dave!"

"You're right," he said. "It won't."

"Wrong," said Myra. "I don't think Uncle Dave has a choice."

"What do you mean?"

"A choice that the Chaos Theory contract should make much easier," chimed in Stein. He produced a ten-page stapled document out of seemingly nowhere. "Paperwork for the use of your house. The $160,000 is a standard amount, you can check around."

Dave stared numbly at the contract, but only for a second. "O-kay...But we don't have to do this."

Chuck and Rashid re-appeared at that moment, nodded at Myra to signal the house was safe. She nodded back and began to pace.

"Let's talk about *your* reality show, Mr. Dunwoody. Abducting and transporting a woman without her consent across state lines, harboring her in your house and now, from what I've been hearing, lying and misrepresenting yourselves as paid caregivers to her is not going to fly too high with the media or state law enforcement." She held up her cell phone. "Which I now have on speed dial."

"But that's not what happened," pleaded Dave, "I told you. The whole thing is just a big coincidence that snowball—"

"You also stand to lose custody of your two nieces."

Dave, Trish and Fran glanced at each other in sheer horror.

"Yes, I made a few extra calls yesterday...Uncle Dave."

* * *

On the floor of his van, Monty was brought back to consciousness by the sound of voices. He painfully sat up. The voices belonged to young men, and one of them was laughing. Monty remembered where he was parked and climbed into the driver's seat, looked in the side mirror. Saw the vans from Omaha A/V Rentals in front of the Dunwoody house and nearly had a stroke. He grabbed the nearest camera and telephoto lens, slung some film canisters over his shoulder and jumped out in the street.

A young grip smoking a cigarette in the passenger seat of the first van saw Monty coming and put down the window.

"Can we help you?"

"Maybe. What's all this about, mate?"

The grip shared an amused glance with his cohort behind the wheel. "Nothing you need to know about, sir."

"Well, if this is about Normandie Vine I sure as damn well should. You got a bloomin' clue who I am?"

"Yeah, a local drunk who's trying to piss me off. Take a walk, okay?"

Monty screwed on his biggest lens, cocked the camera like a shotgun. The side of the van slid open and a third A/V guy who was even bigger and scarier-looking than Monty stepped out.

"Get that telephoto out of here, buzzard, before I use it for your next colonoscopy."

Monty sputtered and swore at the asphalt, but retreated to his van, firing off a few shots of the Dunwoody house as he went.

* * *

Trish and Fran had Dave cornered in the kitchen. Three feet away on the table lay the papers he had just signed, and Paul Stein was already having an assistant snap pictures of the room with his phone.

"I'm not trying to tear anything apart," said Dave, doing his best to keep his voice down.

"Yes you are!" cried Fran, "First you get a big creepy crush on her and now you're just going to sell her out to these leeches?"

"You'd rather lose me as your guardian? And the more I think about it...Damn... 160 grand could sure put you guys through college."

"Screw college! I'm gonna volunteer in a homeless suicide drug rehab transgender halfway house and horse stable anyway, and you probably just blew my resumé for that."

"That's unfortunate, Frannie. Really. Because your parents sure wanted the best for you."

Fran turned away and pounded her leg with a balled-up little fist.

"That wasn't nice," said Trish.

"Okay, I'm sorry. But come on. We weren't even real deprogrammers. It was a very smart idea, Fran, to get us out of a jam, but we were lying to her."

"It was just wanting the best for someone, Dave!" Fran started to cry, but caught herself and stormed down the hall instead.

"We could have discussed this contract thing a little longer before you grabbed their pen," added Trish.

"You heard the woman, Trish. A little longer? With state police one speed call away? I don't think so. Now can you please talk to your sister so we can maybe get through this thing with at least a minimum of enjoyment?"

"You don't make it sound all that fun."

"Well, maybe it can be. You know, if I've learned anything in the last ten years, it's that you control the things you can, and deal with the things you can't. And damn...the Dunwoodys getting on TV doesn't happen every day, right?" Trish's simmering face cooled a little, but she was anything but overjoyed.

Outside the kitchen door, Myra stood with Normandie, who looked cold and very jumpy.

"You all right, hon?"

"I don't know...I mean—I don't know about this."

"Sure you do."

"Reality shows blow, Myra."

"Ssh! Come here..." Myra walked her around the side of the house, within view of the murky backyard pond.

"Charming...Anyway, what you need, hon, is to reconnect with your fans. Not just these yahoos. With your global base—"

"Don't call them yahoos. Okay, they were pulling my chain a little, but at least they're nice. And I could certainly use more nice."

"Paul Stein will slam dunk the nice, know why? Because he's a genius. Trust me, this show is going to spin the globe."

Normandie sighed. "So what's our fake story again? I survived two days alone in the Colorado mountains...before two of my biggest fans came across me while on a hike...then took me in like some frickin' wounded doe? Who's gonna believe that?"

"People believe anything they're told on TV, Normie."

"It just doesn't feel right—"

"Of course not. But it's entertainment. Here..." She reached in her bag again. "I even brought you a new Mother Nature's bar." She handed her the familiar health snack. Like the one at Peak Experience, this one also had a mysterious open slit on the side.

Back in the house, Paul Stein had taken a flustered Dave aside.

"You have cooked a turkey before, correct? Because we'll be happy to provide one."

"No, that's okay. I'd rather cook my own. And my nieces make a mean stuff—"

"Super. We'll be paying for all the groceries you need, of course." He turned to Myra as she came back in. "When can Amwolf get here?"

"First thing tomorrow, I've been told!"

"Amwolf?" asked Dave.

"Only the most brilliant music video director in Austria," cooed Myra. "You can thank me later."

"And we do need to be strict about those terms of disclosure you signed off on, Dave. I assume you read that paragraph?"

"Uhh, I think I—"

"No word about this show to anyone," said Myra, emphasizing the point with a talon-like finger, "The tighter we keep the lid on the pot, the more delicious the soup's going to be. So hush-hush, sweet Dunwoody."

Five minutes later, Trish and Fran stood on the front porch, watching Dave walk the entourage back to their town car. Fran hadn't even bothered to get dressed and her shivering body futilely tried to tell her this.

"I can't believe they're staying at the Wagon Wheel," said Trish, "Bedbugs won't even go near the place."

"I can't believe I came up with that stupid deprogrammer idea. Look at her."

Normandie paused at the Lincoln's open door to turn and give them a woozy, hurt frown before Myra pulled her into the back seat.

"Crap," uttered Fran, "Did you see her eyes?"

"You don't think—"

"I don't know. And I don't wanna." She turned and marched back in the house.

* * *

The Wagon Wheel Go-Tel existed three miles north of town on Route 79-A, on a stretch so remote that tumbleweeds would often collect on the establishment's backside in summer and clog the air conditioners. It didn't even have a wagon wheel out front, though its ten "kozy kabins" were constructed in the round some time during the Eisenhower administration, and to a bleary-eyed Nebraska traveler might have resembled spokes on a wheel before bossy prairie grass muscled in on the grounds.

A mainly mute old woman of mixed Cheyenne and Swedish blood named Elsa Blue Lake inherited the place from her oil-drilling grandfather and now lived in the office with her five cats and satellite TV. Like Butchie in town, she was overwhelmed when Paul Stein's three vehicles roared onto the premises earlier and had even brewed up two pots of alleged coffee to take around to the eight rented units in her flowered robe.

Myra shared the cabin closest to the office with Normandie, and by eight that evening, the only thing that curbed her disgust with the lumpy beds, cowboy and Indian lamps, filthy shower curtain and knotty pine walls was a fevered glow she still had about *Thanksgiving with Normandie*.

"We may have to tweak the spin just a hair," she said, seated on the bed facing her client, who was leaning back dreamily against her cracked headboard on a fresh Klonopin high.

"Whatevers…"

"Might be better if they had a flat tire while driving you from Colorado and even in your hungry, delirious condition you helped them change it."

"Sure…"

Stein's assistant had gone out earlier and brought back a dozen Runza sandwiches, and Myra moved Normandie's barely eaten one and wrapping aside to join her on the bed—nearly sagging it to the floor.

"Listen, hon. I know the last week hasn't been easy for you. But this is how big time success happens. You take a dirty, stinky hand-me down and turn it into a goddamn golden fleece." She squeezed Normandie's ankle with hard affection. "And who's the best person to make that happen for Amanda Mushnik?"

Normandie's eyes went from dreamy to slightly glazed over.

"Myra is…"

"Remember Santa Paula?"

"I guess…"

"Where you hitchhiked after winning Ojai and no one had a

clue where you went except me? Know why? Because taking care of Normandie is my job. Yeah, I never forgot that Disneyland story your music teacher told me. Or that Santa Paula, right on the way to Ojai, had the same cutesy Victorians up and down the street, with their lame, falling-apart porches you were probably sitting on...And you sure damn were."

Normandie was trying her best to focus, but it was another struggle.

"I just wanted to be alone after the performance..."

"Oh, I knew that." She briefly put an arm around her. "You and Greta Garbo."

"Who?"

"Forget it."

"This 160 grand the Dunwoodys are getting for using their house. It's mostly the reward money?"

"Nope. Chaos Theory's. Looks like we saved Rondo Moroni a nice hunk of change, right?"

Normandie paused a moment to process that.

"Yeah..."

* * *

Back at the house, Dave was loading dirty clothes in the washing machine. He paused to clutch Trish's old Nebraska Cornhusker sweatshirt, which Normandie had been wearing under a coat when they danced out at Mount Loup. Instinctively brought it to his face and sniffed it. Trish popped her head in the laundry room at that second and he dropped the sweatshirt in the washer.

"Hey Uncle Dave. You seen Fran?"

"Um, no. Maybe she went to feed Maynard's horses."

"Not tonight. Maynard's home. Well...maybe she went out for a walk. She was awful upset about this thing."

"Right..."

He stood there with the laundry basket until she walked away, then peered back in the washer for a long moment and reached for the detergent.

* * *

It took Fran a half hour to dig her old cruiser bike out of storage, wipe off the cobwebs and pump up the tires, and then another ninety minutes or so to ride it from Poplar Avenue to the Wagon Wheel. She probably could have borrowed Dana's bike, but that may have meant a hundred more questions and frantic pleas for inclusion, and she did want to honor Myra Harp's "hush clause" if possible.

She had smartly worn winter gloves, and a knit hat inside her bike helmet, but those weren't much help against the icy November wind blowing in from the north. By the time she reached the Wagon Wheel, her lips were numb and her thighs felt like a Camaro's pistons.

She laid her bike on the ground a few yards from the place and made her way alongside the cabins, trying to peer into each one. Two of the crew guys were drinking beers and playing *Gears of War* on an X-box one of them had apparently brought. In another, a third crew member was making out with a skanky girl who may have been on the crew but was likely from Omaha.

Then she saw Normandie through a crack under the blinds of the cabin nearest the office. She lay on her side on one of the beds, Myra beside her and massaging one of Normandie's bare ankles.

Rage filled Fran at that moment. Her long resentment of Myra and growing distrust of the destructive celebrity culture, the hurt of having a new understanding friend yanked away without warning, a weird, fresh passion Fran had barely flirted with in her dreams... All of it mixed with the embedded sorrow she and her sister still felt about losing Mom and Dad, and caused her to look down at the ground and pick up a large rock.

She peeled off one of her gloves and lightly tossed the weapon into the air with her bare hand, gripping the thing a bit tigher every time she caught it. She turned sideways, eyes filling up, reared back with her arm and prepared to fire the rock straight through the window and off Myra's leechy head.

But maybe Uncle Dave is right, she thought. *We can use the money. The Dunwoodys being on TV can't be the worst thing in the world, and the three of us would all get to stay together. Dave wasn't exactly Mom and Dad, but he did uncle his ass off.* Plus, Fran knew she was better than this: hurling a drive-by rock, for God's sake. She let it fall to the ground before pulling her wool glove back on and trudging back to her bike.

CHAPTER FOURTEEN:
CAREER OPPORTUNITIES

Dana had met a kid in Kearney a year or so ago who worked in a combination office printing and T-shirt store, and had no qualms about hitting him up for a giant rush order. Which was why a winded Dana arrived at Googy's on his bike when the market opened at 7 a.m., a bulging canvas bag over his shoulder, and began setting up his business outside the door.

AUTHENTIC "ME 'N' NORMANDIE" SELFIE ART! screamed the Sharpie-markered sign over the display postcards, posters, and mounted T-shirts (SM-M-L-XL) featuring the same selfie photo he had snapped of them at school and enhanced on his computer. A few housewives, farmers, and students ducking in for classroom snacks had already paused to take in the display.

"That the same godless drug addict who's been on TV?" asked local religious fanatic Jason Reimer in his knee-length rubber boots and bright green parka.

"Sure is, Mr. Reimer!" beamed Dana. "Only twelve dollars a shirt."

Reimer waved him off and went inside. An exiting sophmore Dana recognized seemed much more impressed.

"Wow. These are the shit. How'd you fake that photo?"

"Who said I did?"

A few more passing souls stopped to look his wares over, and there was suddenly a tiny crowd. At that moment, Meg Strump came out of Googy's clutching her bagged daily pint and lit up a fresh Marlboro. Plucked one of Dana's postcards off the rack and put it up to her bleary eyes.

"Hey! Met her the other day!" She turned and addressed the small audience. "Staying right across the street from me at the Dunwoodys." Looked back at Dana. "You know her too?"

Dana nodded with pride and Meg wandered back toward the road.

* * *

Cookie and two of the Monsters were holding court in their corner of the school cafeteria when Irene buzzed over to the table, beyond excited.

"Hot take, bitches. Normandie Vine is still at the Dunwoodys, and there's freaking camera crews there."

"Says who?" asked Cookie.

"Says a kid I know who knows another kid, who knows another kid who said Dana was outside Googy's today with a freaking Normandie souvenir stand, that's who."

Cookie pulverized a celery stick with her front teeth. "They lied to us. I knew it. Who's the camera crew? TV news?"

"Maybe. I don't know. There's another kid I know going up there to check it out and she said she'd text me."

"Screw that," said Lakota, "Let's go ourselves."

"Hey wait," said Cookie, "We have to strategize."

"About what?"

"Are you guys idiots? The reward money! Far as I know, that booty is still up for grabs, and we sure as shit still deserve some."

"So strategize, Cook. We'll check in later."

She walked away with Irene and Paula, leaving Cookie at the table with her scheming, baking eyes.

* * *

Trish was eagerly helping the cutest grip on the crew set up a floodlight in the living room when Dave came in and peered out the front curtain.

"Uh-oh. Looks like somebody talked."

Outside, about a dozen town residents had congregated in the road and across the street from the house. Meg was already shooing a few of them off her lawn.

"What's the big deal?" asked Trish.

"Might not be one. But I think they oughta know about it." He turned away from the window in search of his phone.

* * *

While Normandie was in her Wagon Wheel bathroom, showering and dressing in a semi-haze, Stein sat in the adjacent room with Myra, frustratingly trying to find Wall Street news on the place's 1980s-style TV.

"Give it a rest, Paul," said Myra. "It doesn't even have a shopping channel."

Her phone rang. She grabbed it.

"Good morning, Dave! How's the family do—" Her expression twisted. "No kidding. And how did that happen?...Oh. Podunk town, right. Thanks for the tip, Dave. See you soon." She tossed the phone on the bed and looked at Stein, who knew from her face what had happened.

"It's out?"

"Geeks across the street already."

"Great. Think we can contain it?"

"Deny, deny, and deny again, babe."

Someone knocked loudly on the door.

"Now what?" Stein walked over and tried to look through the peephole but it was hopelessly clogged with a gunky cobweb. He cursed and swung the door open.

Monty Matilda stood there with an ear-to-ear grin, holding up a page he'd brought up on his tablet. It was the lead story on DailyWorldNews.com:

NUTTY NORMANDIE IN NEBRASKA!!

Complete with Monty's snapshot of Dave and Normandie dancing to Milton Brown and His Musical Brownies below Mt. Loup.

"Hot off the Interweb, mates!"

"You bastard!" yelled Myra, "I'll SUE you!"

"Have fun with that!" Monty yelled back, backpedaling to his van. Rashid flew in out of nowhere, decked him in the mouth with a punch but he bounced back up and continued on without ever dropping his tablet.

Stein slammed the door shut and turned to Myra, looking like he'd lost every tee time at the Riviera for the rest of the year. "Now THAT we cannot contain!"

Myra thought for a second, and her eyes squinted. A spanking new scheme was formulating.

"So maybe we don't. Maybe we go commando here."

"Without underwear? I don't think—"

"No, no. Who do you know at the networks? Including the cable ones?"

He gave her a scoffing laugh. "I know everyone, Myra."

She stood and began to pace. "Okay then. What if we pitch this as a live event? Change the title and treat it like breaking goddamn news! If Amwolf gets his Austrian ass here today we can grab some grocery shopping footage. I will promise you the first-born son I will never have that every Nielsen rating on the planet will be obliterated."

Stein gave her a slow, glowing nod, and was already reaching for his phone.

* * *

To no one's surprise, Googy's Market just wasn't prepared. Even July 4th threw them into a tizzy, when they were out of charcoal and burger patties well before noon. This time, an invasion of two vans of Omaha filming equipment, two new ones from Kreative Katering and Speedie Makeovers, four "cast" members, a manager, producer, young jet-lagged Austrian director and a good slice of Endeavor's population outside had severely tested Googy Philson's sanity.

Googy, the 60-year-old market matron who wore a butcher's apron that she never used or took off, stood at one of the two registers like General Lee at Fredericksburg, commanding her two beleaguered stock boys and assistant checkout girl with mere points of her finger. She had added some out-of-place rouge to her sagging cheeks for the special occasion, and tried not to glance out at many of her regular customers trapped in the parking lot. Sure, the rumor-stoked gaggle was roped off by Chuck and Rashid a yard or so from the entrance, but they still gawked in wonder and some kind of desire at the otherworldly camera lights through the market's fogged-up windows. The GOOGY'S CLOSED FOR EMERGENCY INVENTORY sign on the door wasn't all that convincing.

Dana had his Normandie wares set up again, and was on the verge of selling them out. A half dozen younger Normandie fans had ditched their fifth grade class to stand in the cold with makeshift autograph books while three-quarters of the Cookie Monsters just sat on Lakota's car hood in the background like sneering ravens.

Chief Gilmore pulled his cruiser right up to the entrance and was met by Chuck.

"Howdy!" said the chief, "You all got a permit to be doing this?"

Chuck immediately went on his shoulder mic.

"Got a local cop out here." He paused to listen for an answer in his earpiece. "Understood." He reached into his suit jacket, took out a blue envelope from Chaos Theory productions and handed it to Gilmore. "Appreciate your help, officer."

The chief peered inside at a collection of fifty-dollar bills. Gave Chuck a friendly salute and drove away.

Inside, Normandie pushed a shopping cart through the produce section with pretend enthusiasm. The Speedie Makeover people had re-fashioned her chopped hair into a fun but edgy arrangement speckled with magenta, and had noticeably enlivened her face. Trish, Fran, and Dave, garbed in their best casual clothes though more neglected in the makeup department, flanked Normandie on both sides as they walked, adding carrots, celery, onions, and parsley to the half-filled cart for the sixth time in the last five minutes.

"Ein more time, bitte!" barked Amwolf Grün, all of 24 years old and fresh out of Berlin's Met Film School. He was amped up on something decidedly illegal to cure his jet lag, and even though these were just "remotes" to insert into the live broadcast scheduled for the next day, Amwolf couldn't help treating them like Christopher Nolan takes from *Inception*, his shock of egg-colored hair flopping over the rest of his short brown scalp like a barn door in a cyclone.

"I gotta pee," announced Normandie to the crew. Normally that would be a signal that she was about to sit in the bathroom and play on her phone for twenty minutes, but Myra hadn't returned her device as of yet, so this was likely the real deal. While Rashid walked her to the tiny, barely clean room in back of the market, Fran allowed one of the Speedie Makeover girls to rush in and do a little hair trimming above her ear.

"Mess with my sideburn and you'll be wearing your ass for a hat," said Fran.

Dave seemed nervous but in a giddy way, and couldn't help peering through the camera at every break.

Trish merely watched Myra as she whispered to Stein, checked and re-checked her phone, whispered to Amwolf, and cut her gaze into every corner of the market with chilling precision. It seared Rashid from ten yards away and he turned to knock on the bathroom door.

"Myra wants you out in less than a minute, Ms. Vine!"

A toilet flushed, and she was back out in fifteen seconds. Trish took note of that too and nudged her sister.

"She isn't Amanda anymore, but she sure as heck doesn't seem like Normandie."

"Yeah," said Fran, "Dollars to Ring-Dings she's on drugs again, but I think it's more than that."

"Like what?"

"Like Myra having this weird mind control thing over her. Normandie may as well be a poodle."

"Rock 'n roll!" she cried out of nowhere, an unsettling gleam in her eyes, "Let's get this shot, Amway!"

"It is Amwolf."

"Whatevers..."

"Gut. Again, bitte!"

The crew hurried back into place. Trish returned to her spot behind the cart. Fran joined her after trying to glance out the window.

"Is Dana still in the parking lot?"

"He was the last time I looked."

"I say we invite him over later. Y'know, after we're done with this 20-ring circus here."

"Invite him for what?"

"Whaddya think? Operation Rescue Overtime. There's a damn Rosemead somewhere in her life and we gotta find that thing."

* * *

The Googy's shoot lasted until two in the afternoon, mainly because Amwolf insisted on perfection for a turkey-ordering moment with Googy herself, even though the actual bird was already being shipped from a farm west of Minneapolis.

While Normandie headed back to the Wagon Wheel with Myra and the crew, Dave drove to the animal clinic to put in a few hours of work. He was startled to see Patty exiting the building as he arrived, carrying two of her plants. There was rage on her face and she'd been crying.

"Uh-oh," said Dave.

"Too late," she replied, fumbling for the keys to her muddy Dodge pickup. "I know where you'd rather put your attention."

"What are you talking about? You're quitting?"

She paused at the door of her vehicle. "I stopped at Googy's on my way in this morning. And I saw you inside getting all famous with your 'out-of-town guest'. Fine. Just don't pretend you give a good darn about me or this clinic."

"Patty, I'm sorry. I meant to call but it's just been a crazy whirlwind."

"Oh, it sure has. And now I'll just be blowing away. Have fun with your waiting room."

"Patty, c'mon. Don't leave."

She slammed the truck closed, gunned the engine and drove away. Dave trudged inside the clinic, took one look at the half dozen townsfolk sitting with their assorted pets and staring him down, and his entire body slumped.

* * *

In the Dunwoody garage, Trish, Fran, and Dana had every plastic tub of Normandie clippings dumped out on the floor.

"This is like building the New York subway system out of Legos," moaned Trish.

"Or at least Chicago's," added Fran.

"Hey," said Dana, "I'm losing possible sales just being here, so maybe we try to focus?"

"Good idea," said Fran. "You start."

"Okay." He grabbed a folder of clippings and thumbed through them. "First of all, when was her first big drug bust again? I mean, the one that started the spiral?"

"Why that?"

"Because Normandie was never this spaced out and walking around like a Myrabot before, right? You guys said yourself she never had any major boyfriends or huge breakups. So when was the bust?"

"I'm not sure," said Fran, "2011 maybe?"

"Around when she cancelled her Salt Lake City show..." Dana squinted out a thought. "Why did she cancel again?"

"Hold on, saw that the other day..." Trish located a handful of clippings off to the side from that year. Dug through them and found the one she wanted.

"Says here she came down with a 24-hour stomach flu. 'Ms. Vine went for a morning hike to clear her head and it hit her like a truck when she returned to the hotel' said a spokesperson who sure sounds like Myra."

"Okay..." said Dana, "But didn't she also cancel a show in Dallas after that?"

"Right!" chimed in Trish, "Meaning the 24-hour bug thing could have been bogus." They all looked at each other. Fran quickly grabbed a nearby torn-out page from an entertainment rag.

"And two weeks after that she was arrested on that flight to Paris for snorting up in the plane's restroom before takeoff. Which started everything."

"Something happened in Salt Lake," said Trish.

"Or on that hike," said Dana.

There were at least five seconds of silent conjecture.

"Panic attack?" wondered Fran. "She sure didn't do too well in the Colorado woods the other day."

"Maybe Myra can tell us," offered Trish.

"Right. And maybe O.J. can tell us what happened to Nicole."

"Why not ask Normandie?" said Dana.

Fran shook her head dismissively. "All we know is that Myra Harp practically became her guardian after this Sofia was out of the picture a long time ago, and now she's basically her Dr. Frankenstein and Mother Superior."

"Isn't that just being a dedicated manager?"

"Yeah, but something must have happened…"

Dana zipped up his jacket and reached for his bike helmet.

"Where are you going?" asked Fran.

"Home for further online research. Plus I have a term paper to finish for Physics—if there's time for that."

He left the garage. Trish looked at Fran.

"Maybe he's right."

"About what?"

"His idea."

"Writing a term paper?"

"No, the first one. About asking Normandie."

Somewhat out of character, she gave Fran a sly grin.

* * *

Dave had retrieved an old can of Coors he had stashed in a gym bag in back of his closet. His deceased brother had been trying to get him off booze for years, and the shame he felt after the crash soon had him hiding bottles and cans around like forbidden Easter eggs. He was now drinking this one warm in his armchair, staring numbly at a segment of *Celebrities Tonight* that was hosted by some smiling, busty hairdo.

"That's right, Dan! Normandie Nation was stunned to learn that

their idol had not escaped or been abducted from her high-priced mental health spa in the Rockies, but had actually been rescued and taken in by a broken but all-American Nebraska family! Well, the world can meet the Dunwoodys tomorrow on 'A Pre-Thanksgiving with Normandie', a live reality event on the highly-rated People's Pleasure Network—"

He killed the set as Trish and Fran appeared in the doorway with their hoodies on.

"Hey Uncle Dave," said Trish, "We have to go pick up a few more things for the stuffing tomorrow."

"Okay..."

"You all right?"

"Actually, no. I had to fix a cat's ear, a dog's tooth, a parakeet's wing, and a rabbit's foot in an hour and a half without anyone to help me."

"Oh man...We're sorry. You don't think Patty will come back?"

"Sure not counting on it..." He finished off his beer and dropped the empty can in his lap. "Shoot, what have I done? Maybe this whole thing with Normandie is a mistake."

"Well, you did already sign the papers," said Fran.

"We'll help you get through it, Uncle Dave," said Trish.

"Yeah. Just don't drink too much of that strong stuff."

* * *

Twenty minutes later, Trish pulled the Focus into the Wagon Wheel's driveway and killed the lights.

"Think Elsa Blue Lake is asleep?" asked Trish.

"She was last night," said Fran.

They both seemed nervous. Trish backed the car around near the entrance so they were facing the main road, and they climbed out, throwing their hoods over their heads.

The tall grass on the backside of the cabin was a minefield of broken bottles, empty chip bags, and a few soiled diapers, and Trish and Fran had to tiptoe through them to approach the slatted bathroom window. Fran inched up to it and peered through two of the slats.

Normandie lay in a bubble bath with a washcloth over her face. Fran was somewhat transfixed by this, and Trish poked her from behind.

"See her?"

Fran nodded, but seemed uncertain what to do next. "Isn't this where we throw pebbles or something?"

"That's a two or three floors down thing, Fran. And usually a guy thing."

"Right..." She braced herself with a deep breath and gently rapped on the glass slats. Normandie didn't move. Fran noticed that she was thankfully not wearing any earbuds and knocked a bit louder.

"Normandie!" Fran half-whispered.

This time Normandie paused, then peeled the washcloth off her face. Bunched her brow. Fran tried another knock. Normandie scooped a towel off the floor, stood, wrapped it around her and climbed out of the tub. Dripped her way to the window.

"Who's out there?"

"Just us!"

She opened the slats and was startled to see Fran's shivering face inside her hoodie.

"Hi Normandie. We don't mean to bug ya. Really. But something's been bugging us and we figured there wouldn't be any time to talk tomorrow."

"Hell yeah about that. But why should I help a bunch of frauds?" She blew a small cloud of soap bubbles off her nose.

"Well..."

Trish seized power for a change and stepped in front of her. "We just noticed that Myra seems to go all Jedi mind trick on you lots of the time. Like you're not yourself as much around her."

Normandie stared out at the dark plains for a moment, then shrugged. "That's your opinion."

"So...nothing ever happened between you two?" asked Fran, "Like when she first saw you in Ojai?"

"Or Salt Lake City?" piped in Trish, "When you cancelled that concert?"

Normandie froze for a second, then looked at the girls with fresh paranoia.

"Why are you doing this?"

"Doing what?"

"Giving me the third degree. I don't even like second degrees."

"Well...maybe because we care about you."

"We both do," added Fran.

"You're just so talented, Normandie," said Trish, struggling to keep her voice down, "and it's such a gift to be talented. Crap, even to just be inspired. Look at me with my dopey karaoke videos. I'm just a high school junior nobody knows trying to get through the day and do you know how much even one of those videos I do picks me up?"

Fran tapped her sister's shoulder. Not just to quiet her down a bit, but because Chuck and Rashid were a cabin away, slowly moving toward them.

"Uhh...Trish?"

"We met Amanda the other day," Trish continued, oblivious, "and that's who you are. We really liked her. And Amanda wouldn't be doing any baloney reality show—"

"RUN!" yelled Fran. Trish whirled, saw the two bodyguards bounding through the high grass, and bolted in the opposite direction. Normandie quickly shut the slats. Chuck tripped over a discarded 12-pack of beer bottles. Rashid tried to dodge him but had to bounce off the side of the cabin to do so, giving Trish and Fran an opening to race back around to the road with their hoods still on tight.

"That sure went well," said Fran, out of breath.

Myra knocked on the bathroom door seconds later, then opened it and saw Normandie in the bubble bath, washcloth back on her face.

"What the hell was that?"

"Oh...Couple of locals wanting autographs."

Myra hissed under her breath, shut the door again. "Vermin..."

* * *

Hours later, prairie winds had picked up, and Normandie was having trouble sleeping. She got out of bed, felt her way through the dark around to Myra's night table.

Myra's phone and plugged-in earbuds were right next to her Vicodin. She silently took the phone and the buds, went back to her bed and ducked under the covers with them. Popped in the earbuds, then went to YouTube and typed TRISH DUNWOODY THE FEAR into the search window. She unearthed the barely-viewed video, cranked the volume a few notches, and listened to more of Trish's rendition of the Lily Allen song:

Life's about film stars and less about mothers
It's all about fast cars and cussing each other
But it doesn't matter cause I'm packing plastic
And that's what makes my life so fucking fantastic

And I am a weapon of massive consumption
And it's not my fault it's how I'm programmed to function
I'll look at the sun and I'll look in the mirror
I'm on the right track, yeah we're on to a winner

As the chorus began, genuine tears began to well in Normandie's eyes.

I don't know what's right and what's real anymore
And I don't know how I'm meant to feel anymore
And when do you think it will all become clear?
Cause I'm being taken over by the fear

She killed the video, wiped both of her eyes dry with part of the sheet. Then she went back on the phone and scrolled through Myra's contacts. Stopped on the listing for Rondo Moroni. Saw his long phone number in Italy and gazed at it for a very long time.

CHAPTER FIFTEEN:
COLD TURKEY

Meg Strump rifled through her kitchen drawers. The knife she used to slice open watermelons during the summer might have worked, but that one was a bit long and thin, and for a situation like this she needed something scary. After climbing a stool and reaching above the stove, she came down with Rudy Strump's dust-covered set of steak knives, and summarily extracted the one he used to carve the top sirloin the night he fatally keeled over in front of the Rasmussens.

None of the two dozen vehicles clogging Poplar Avenue had as much as tickled her property yet, but the day was young, and she wasn't taking chances. Clear-headed before noon for a change, Meg dragged a lawn chair out to the curb and parked herself on it, brandishing Rudy's carving knife.

"Touch my yard and I murder your tires, you barbarians!" she shouted. The flood of locals merely grinned, but a few of the sixty or so media members and photographers on hand inched away from her yard. Monty, naturally, had muscled his way to the front of the paparazzi mob stationed on the Dunwoody sidewalk, his lower lip still plum-like from Rashid's fist.

Inside the house amidst a blizzard of pre-shoot activity, an assistant rapped on the bathroom door. Hearing no response, she flagged down a passing grip.

"Who's in there? Normandie?"

"Probably," said the grip, and kept moving.

This time it was actually Fran standing at the bathroom mirror, garbed in a too-tight orange sweater with little brown turkeys on it that made her vaguely resemble a pockmarked pumpkin. Despite wearing more makeup on her face than a Vegas showgirl, her expression was the epitome of glum. She remembered something, took out her phone, and found the photo of comatose Normandie in her bed she had snapped that first night.

"You can do this, Fran..." she muttered, "One shitty hour and it's over."

She sighed, then picked up a plastic water bottle she had dumped out and re-filled with red wine. Unscrewed the top and drank nearly half of it.

"I don't care how bad your meter reading is, knives and spoons go on the right side around here." It was Trish, giving her new lighting chum a hard time about the dinner settings. A cheesy, flower-emroidered cloth had been laid over a long folding table that took up most of the living room. Brown candles, a ceramic turkey, and centerpiece arrangement of daisies, burnt orange roses, hydrangea and sunflowers were perfectly positioned. Seating had also been arranged, with Dave and Normandie name cards at the far ends and the sisters across from each other in the middle.

"I hear you," said the lighting guy, "but the way the cameras and lights are positioned, there's just too much glare."

"So move the cameras or the lights!" replied Trish with a playful grin. One of the two cameramen stood nearby with a steadicam strapped to his body, curbing his aggravation.

Dave, meanwhile, was boxed into a corner of the living room with Amwolf and the second camera operator, who was shooting an "on-the-fly" candid to insert later.

"It's really, really an honor to have Normandie Vine here," he said into the camera as naturally as he could manage. He wore a stiff white dress shirt under the only sport jacket he owned, a camel corduroy blazer with dark brown shoulder patches. "She's a great girl and my nieces tell me she's pretty talented, though I've never heard her music."

Off camera, Amwolf read from a list of questions someone had put on his phone.

"What opinion do you have on the unfair attitude about Normandie that is in the press worldwide?"

"Well, I'm not sure exactly what attitude you mean, but yeah, it's probably unfair. Because from what I've seen, she's sweet, and funny, and she can sure dance."

"Like a substitute for your late sister-in-law I must think."

Dave froze. The starter wrinkles under his eyes quivered.

"Not at all...No. I wouldn't say that."

"You misunderstand. What I mean was—"

"Jean was an angel. She lit up the house and loved my brother more than anything."

"I am sorry, David. Why don't we—

"I always looked forward to coming over for Thanksgiving...Every year." He leaned forward and clutched Amwolf's pale wrist. "Cliff and Jean are always here on Thanksgiving, okay? Even when they aren't."

He rose and walked away. Amwolf shook his head and gave the cameraman a throat-cutting gesture.

"We will use his first answer."

In the kitchen, while assistants tripped over themselves trying to position the piping hot serving trays on the counter, Normandie was by the back door with a wardobe person. She wore a bright yellow party dress and heels, offsetting her glazed expression, and was flipping through a rack of two dozen aprons. Most were either nondescript or hideous.

"No...No...No...Too Martha ...No...No...Not Martha enough... No..." She stopped and pulled one out sporting a "woodcut" image of Native Americans and pilgrims shaking hands. Her face brightened. "My people!"

At the kitchen table a few feet away, Myra huddled with Stein while they pored over a shooting schedule on his tablet.

"Amwolf wants to go back to Googy's," mulled Stein, "Says he forgot to get a close-up of Normandie choosing a potato."

"He can fake one here. We're done with that roadside stand." She glanced over at Normandie, who now had her chosen apron on and was modeling it for the crew. "If she can just get through this hour."

"Did you give her...something in a health bar?"

"Oh yes. At least two."

"Good. So I guess we can relax. A holiday toast, a meal, dessert, good G-rated vibes all around will make Normandie Nation sleep like babies tonight, right? And when we see the numbers tomorrow, so will we."

Myra tightened her mouth, unable to lose its sour expression.

"She needs to sing."

"I don't know...Sounds like a challenge."

"I mean it, Paul. She didn't get where she is by ramming police cars. People need to be reminded of that."

"Fine. So which catchy, semi-sleazy Thanksgiving number aimed at 16-year-olds will she perform?"

"Don't be a schmuck."

"I'm being a producer. Either way, you may want to run this idea by Normandie first."

Myra sighed and stood up. "I was afraid you'd say that."

A makeup person was adding some final touches to Normandie's cheek as Myra strolled over.

"Ready to talk some turkey, hon?"

Normandie flashed a smile without looking at her. "You bet."

"Did you have your...appetizers?"

"Uh-huh."

"Listen, Paul thought it would be extra special if you worked a little tune into the menu. What do you think?"

"No prob. Trish and Fran have CDs of mine I forgot I even recorded. I'm sure they can put one on at a low enough vol—"

"No, no. I meant a live number sometime during the meal. Like in one of those old musicals where the lead just breaks into song."

Normandie frowned at her. "Why would I do that?"

"Because I'm asking nicely?"

"Yeah, but this is a reality show, remember? And that's kind of unreal."

"Oh, I know, hon. But your fans would just love it. And after what you put them through this week, don't you think you owe it to them?"

"Eine minute!" yelled Amwolf.

Normandie half-nodded at Myra, but her mind had clearly gone down river.

"Where's Fran??" asked Trish, spinning around. The bathroom door in the hall opened at that instant and her sister finally emerged. Fran had washed all the makeup off her face and spiked up her hair even more with half a tub of gel.

Crew members cleared out of the living room except for Amwolf and the two steadicam guys. Dave moved behind the chair at the head of the table and jitterly poured himself a glass of Korbel. Trish poured sparkling apple juice for her and Fran, and when Normandie pointed to her empty glass, one for her too.

Outside, so many people covered the Dunwoody lawn you couldn't see the grass. Most were trying to peer through the windows but those who couldn't were busy taking selfies with the house behind them. Another growing mob clustered around the open side door of an Omaha A/V Rental van, where a monitor was set up and running a live feed of the People's Pleasure Network. Yesterday's slam-edited shopping sequence from Googy's was airing as an intro.

"All gut?" Amwolf asked the room, strapping on a pair of headsets. His assistant director gave him a thumbs-up. Normandie fidgeted with the lapel mic affixed to the breast of her party dress, gave her chopped mane an obligatory toss, took a deep breath and winked at Amwolf. The assistant director checked an app on his phone and raised a megaphone that wasn't really needed.

"And we're live in 5...4...3...2...1." A green light blinked atop Steadicam-1 and he pointed a finger at Normandie.

"Hi everyone!" Normandie beamed, as if a Coleman lantern had just switched on inside her. "Normandie here, in case you don't remember me, and I am just stoked to the maximum gills to be having Thanksgiving today with the Dunwoodys in Endeavor, Nebraska!"

A few dopey crewpeople hooted and hollered. Trish and Dave dutifully applauded. Fran flashed a two-finger peace sign at the camera and did a tepid gangsta roll of her upper torso.

"Should we start off with a toast?" asked Trish.

"There there!" said Normandie, and raised her glass of sparkling apple juice. Trish cleared her throat.

"To our favorite musician and actress in the world, who we are so fortunate to have saved from the wild Colorado wilderness a few days ago!"

"O-kay!" said Normandie. She began to sip from her glass but paused when Dave also cleared his throat.

"To our exciting new friend, and to everyone watching around the world, and to everyone here today...and to those who couldn't —" His eyes began to tear up.

"Word!" cried Fran. Hurriedly clinked his glass and everyone drank.

"Cool," said Normandie, "Who wants to help me bring in the grub?"

"I will!" chirped Trish, and shot into the kitchen with her, Steadicam-2 on their heels. Amwolf rushed over to Fran with Steadicam-1.

"Can we shoot quick OTF of you now?"

"Hell no Rudolph. Later."

"It is Amwolf, bitte."

"Well, bitte my ass."

* * *

Down at Googy's Market, Googy stood with a dozen or so shoppers in the Scoop-a-Loop, watching the show on Cyril's little TV.

"Hard to believe that girl was just shopping here yesterday," said a customer.

"And I can't believe how small she was in person," added Googy.

"Everyone looks mightier on a screen!" piped up Jayson Reimer, "It's the Lord's way of pulling our pants down!"

* * *

Over at the Broken Burro, the afternoon cervezas crowd was also glued to the broadcast, despite the sound being drowned out by laughter, Spanish chatter, and the ever-present jukebox salsa.

* * *

Meanwhile, Dana was one of three students who bothered to show up for Mr. Pumberton's English class. The senile, half-deaf instructor copied an Emerson poem on the chalkboard at an agonizingly slow speed, enabling Dana to surf from one web page to another on his laptop in the back row. When he suddenly landed on a *Salt Lake Tribune* page and began reading the type, an 1840s goldpanner's smile seized his face.

"Ka-ching..."

With barely a look in Mr. Pumberton's direction he shut his laptop, dropped it in his backpack and slipped out of the room.

* * *

In the kitchen, Normandie hovered one inch over the baking dish of stuffing, smelling it in.

"Hot dang! Nothing like a food coma, right? You guys made this?"

"Sure did!" replied Trish.

Normandie plucked a hunk of it out with her finger and Trish playfully swatted her hand away.

"Comin' through, guys!" A burly assistant lifted the turkey out of the oven wearing oven mitts and set it on the counter beside them.

"Shazang!" said Normandie, "Who's gonna Texas chainsaw this bad boy?"

"I guess that would be my uncle," said Fran.

A minute or so later in the living toom, Dave stood paralyzed in front of the turkey, holding a giant fork and electric carving knife. The knife was silent. You could hear a clock ticking in the den a full room away.

"Go for it, Uncle Dave!" said Trish.

"Rock 'n' roll, Dave!" said Normandie.

Fran leaned over and whispered in his ear.

"In case you forgot...Mom always liked white meat, Dad drumsticks."

Dave paused a moment to let his mind curl around the words, then switched on the carving knife, grinned sheepishly at the camera and went to work.

At the edge of the room, Myra anxiously watched a monitor with Stein.

"Cripes. We have a delay on this?"

"Five seconds."

"May want to make it ten."

Dave carved the bird slowly and methodically, stacking a mountain of white meat on an adjacent plate.

"Can't remember the last time I had a meal like this," said Normandie, mainly to break the silence.

"Uhh...last Thanksgiving?" cracked Fran. She had already polished off her sparkling juice and was re-filling her glass with champagne, much to Trish's dismay. "I mean of course, whenever you last went to one, which might've been...at your Aunt Sophie's house, right?"

"Yeah," muttered Normandie, her mind clouding over, "Out in Arcadia. Near L.A." She painfully gathered her wits again, addressed the camera lens that was a few inches from her nose. "Just so everyone's clear, Fran and Trish made the awesome stuffing and I helped with the yams."

Dave finally set the carving knife down, ripped off a turkey leg with his bare hand and dropped it on a second empty plate. He added a half dozen more slabs of white meat to Jean's plate along with a pint of gravy, then slid both plates to an unoccupied corner of the table.

"Dig in, you two!" he said to the empty air.

Trish faked a laugh. "Uncle Dave does this every year!" she exclaimed to whoever was listening, "Makes a few extra plates for homeless people in town!"

"Wow, that is so way beyond cool," said Normandie.

Myra elbowed Stein. "Who was he talking to?"

"His sister-in-law and brother in their graves," whispered Amwolf nearby.

"Are you shitting me? What is this, House of Usher?" She caught Normandie's eye, balled one of her hands into an invisible mic and made a "singing" gesture into it. Normandie looked away a few seconds, then picked up a knife and clinked her glass repeatedly.

"Okay! So now..." She waited until everyone in the room and likely the world was watching her. "Who's gonna say grace?"

Myra rolled her eyes. Dave, Trish, and Fran were tongue-tied. This was clearly not a thing in the Dunwoody house.

"Nobody? Fine. I'll just do Jewish grace then: 'Someone tried to kill us. We survived. Amen.' "

Stein was speechless. Myra was apoplectic. Dave, Trish, and Fran barely even got the joke.

"Great! Let's eat!" blurted Trish, standing and filling her plate. Normandie followed suit, then Fran, and finally Dave, after reluctantly, emotionally sliding his brother's plate back in front of him. Normandie watched him do this and was visibly touched.

* * *

Dana pumped his bike pedals up the hill to Poplar Avenue so hard he threatened to snap them off. He swung around the corner, slammed his brake, skidded the bike the final ten yards and vaulted over a snowbank. Backpack still miraculously on, he bounced to his feet and weaved his way through the crowd at the front porch.

"Excuse me! EXCUSE ME!!"

Rashid was there on the steps to greet him.

"Get lost, skinny man."

"I'm invited to dinner, and I'm late!"

"No you ain't and too damn bad."

"Please! I'm Trish and Fran's best friend!!"

Rashid wouldn't budge, so Dana dove right past him and rammed his knuckles on the front door.

Inside, Amwolf heard the loud knock through his headphones.

"Scheiss..." He motioned to everyone at the table to keep things rolling. It was too late, Trish and Fran had heard the knock too and were standing and looking at the door. Through the curtain, they could see Dana futilely trying to wrestle with Rashid.

"It's Dana!" cried Trish, "Our um...our friend from town!"

"Our homeless friend, actually!" added Fran.

"He's homeless? Well we better let him in then!" announced Normandie. Stein looked at Myra, who just threw up her hands. Fran dashed to the door, swung it open and hauled the breathless, hair-mussed Dana inside. Steadicam 2 zoomed in to capture the moment. Dana wasn't beaming crazily like the first time he walked in on a meal with Normandie; this time he looked dead serious about something.

"Everybody? This is Dana, who lives under the railroad tracks down by the um...by the tracks. He's one of the people our uncle makes a plate of Thanksgiving food for every year."

Dana began to say something contrary and Fran nudged him in the ribs. Walked him to the table and quickly made him a plate less plentiful than the ones Dave had assembled.

"Gee," he said into the camera, after pausing two seconds to tongue-plaster his cowlick, "I am so thankful for this." A grip slid another chair under his butt and he sat down.

"Sometimes we just love taking care of Endeavor's homeless... person," said Fran, "Right, Uncle Dave?" Dave was busy trying to focus on his mouthful of turkey, but managed a nod and weak smile.

"It's awesome you guys do that," said Normandie. Her leg began to bounce nervously under the table. "So...so...awesome. I mean if everyone in the world took care of someone in need like that once a day, or even once a week, hate and fear would just get wiped out. Or at least die in the gutter like crazy dogs."

"Definitely!" said Fran, raising her mash-potatoed fork in solidarity.

Both of Normandie's legs were now bouncing. Her bunched-up

dinner napkin dropped on the floor. She downed her sparkling apple juice and got to her feet.

"Actually, it makes me want to sing!"

"Yes…" said Myra under her breath. A few crewpeople hooted.

Instead, Normandie froze like a stylish icicle in front of her plate.

"Except this time I won't be singing. Because I don't have a song in me. This is no old musical, understand? It's a reality show. It's real life."

Stein shared an anxious look with Myra. Amwolf mumbled in German to himself. A suddenly alarmed Trish glanced down at Normandie's napkin on the floor and saw two unswallowed Klonopins she had spit out inside it. Trish discreetly grabbed them off the floor, rose back up and tried to make eye contact with her sister, but Fran was staring at Normandie, letting her idol's latest words sink in.

"Darn right it's real life!" Trish announced to the room. Dana gave Fran an anxious nudge, and her sister got the hint. "Right…" Fran said, "Speaking of realities, Dana …What's it like down at the homeless camp these days?"

"Oh…cold and miserable as usual. But a person I know there said he knew someone a while ago who may have met you once, Normandie!"

Normandie slowly dropped back in her chair, heart still racing from her little speech but mildly intrigued. "Oh yeah? Met me?"

"Yeah, hold on a sec. I put his name in my phone…" He whipped the cell out of his jacket pocket like a six-shooter and opened an app. "Rex Yardley. Ring a bell?"

A bell would be putting it mildly. Normandie's face turned two shades of pale. Her pupils dilated. A hot mountain gust from a nightmarish past swept across the western plains and broadsided her. She wobbled on the chair. Grabbed hold of the tablecloth and nearly yanked her plate of food into her lap.

"No I…don't know him."

"Are you sure?" Dana probed, "He was a big fan of yours… Maybe the biggest one in Utah in the summer of 2011. I just read an article about him today. Last seen going up Mill Gulch Trail, off Big Cottonwood Canyon Road outside of Salt Lake. That ring a bell?"

Across the room, Myra paced like a rat in a maze. "We need to stop this," she said to Stein. Stein just looked perplexed. "We need to stop this!" she said to Amwolf, who brushed her aside and was transfixed on the table conversation along with the rest of the crew and the world.

"That sounds familiar a little," Normandie said, nervously scratching her hair. She tried to reach for the wine bottle beside Dave but he held it back from her, suddenly alert again and somewhat engaged.

"You did have a thing about heights the other day," he said, "Up on Mt. Loup."

"Yeah, whatever. Can we just talk about the homeless some more?"

"They found Rex Yardley in a gulley below Mill Gulch Trail, Normandie," Dana continued, "The day after you said you were on that same trail."

"I didn't know him."

At Googy's, the Broken Burro, and at numerous Los Angeles bars and restaurants, no one could speak or take their eyes off the screen.

"Rex belonged to every Normandie Vine fan club there was, had a tenth row seat for that night's concert—which you ended up cancelling."

"No one cares about that guy okay? It's old news—"

"Seems that he was telling everyone his mission in life was to marry you, and he sent you a new proposal letter every week—"

"CUT!!" yelled Myra from the shadowy wings, but the crew ignored her.

"Something happened, right?" Dana resumed, out of his chair now, circling the table like an expert trial lawyer, "You cancelled the Salt Lake concert, then one in Dallas, and soon after that you were deep into drugs."

"I said I didn't know this guy!"

"Yeah, but did you see him on the trail? Did he try and take a selfie with you and slip or something? Did you come across his bod—"

"ALRIGHT!!!"

With a frightening primal scream, she tipped over the entire dinner table in an explosion of glasses and china. "HE CAME AT ME WITH THE KNIFE, DAMN IT! WHAT WAS I SUPPOSED TO DO??"

The only sound in the room was a serving bowl of gravy, clattering and spilling across the hardwood floor. There was fear and a bit of madness in Normandie's eyes, yet they were also more alive than we'd ever seen them.

"I just needed some fresh air and exercise and alone time...which is why I took the rental car. But this guy must've followed me up the road and onto the trail. Wearing a tie dye shirt with my face on it, of course...Catches me at the top of this high ridge and says he loves me and wants to give me a baby and when I tell him to get away from me he...takes out a knife and charges—"

Her voice cracked. Myra glanced around in sheer panic. Saw a portable generator on the floor with many things plugged into it— and a grip standing guard and watching her.

"But I kicked out my leg! Hit him in the knee and he slipped and fell...right over the edge. Heard a crack far below which was either his head or his neck on a rock, I don't know. I couldn't look. He even dropped his knife and I grabbed it. Threw it in some lake on the way down I think. Barely remember that part..."

"She's making this up, of course!" snapped Myra, stepping out of the shadows. "Normandie not only sings, she has a great imagination—"

"NO MYRA, YOU DO!!" Normandie's outburst stopped Myra in her vulture-like tracks. "Telling me it didn't happen. Telling people I had the flu. Meanwhile there's some poor confused dude lying dead in a gulley because somehow I made him fall in love with me, or with my brand. Well, guess what?" She strode up to the nearest steadicam and addressed the lens. "Guess what, world? Normandie Vine has recorded her last album, shot her last movie and done her last damn TV appearance, so enjoy the next five minutes."

"See?" resumed Myra, undaunted and rushing up to join her, "She's kidding right now!"

Normandie shoved her violently away with a forearm. One of Myra's pumps slipped in gravy and she crashed to the floor.

"The hell I am, you bloodsucker! I mean, thanks for helping me become a star and all, but you can have it back now. Shit...*Being famous can't hold a candle to knowing who you are.*"

"YES!!"

This shout was from Fran a few feet away, her body shaking, giving in to tears of joy she never knew were in her. She stood over the pre-Thanksgiving rubble, dropped a serving fork that had been in her hand and it clanked off a fallen plate.

"I am so..." She couldn't even finish her sentence. Amwolf normally would have stopped the filming but like everyone else, was too stunned to even react.

"I think I'm..."

In full view of the cameras and global audience she walked up to Normandie and took her around the waist.

"I'm in love with you, Amanda Mushnik."

And planted a wet, passionate kiss on the pop idol's lips. Dave was shocked and moved simultaneously. Trish's hands went up to both sides of her face in Edvard Munch *Scream* fashion. Myra just lay there in the gravy.

"Wow," said Amanda, "Okay to be truthy and all. But whoa—" And Fran kissed her again, this time longer and more intensely.

The epicenter of all that was safe and secure in the world of celebrity erupted in the Dunwoody living room at that moment, sending countless embers of social and corporate media mania into the sky in all directions from its Endeavor, Nebraska volcano. Reporters in front of the house jumped on their cell phones. Nearly everyone else onto their Facebooks or Twitters. The show's worldwide audience broke into gasps, cheers, or Oh. My. Gods.

Myra was having a hard time getting out of her gravy puddle.

Stein was merely out of his mind and getting in Amwolf's face. "You have to cut this!"

"Why?? It is the cinema of history now!"

Trish ran up and embraced Fran and Amanda. Dave began to, but decided to give them their space and instinctively applauded instead. Many of the other crew members did the same.

Then a couple of silverware pieces strewn on the floor began to rattle. The light fixture over the knocked-over table throbbed. Then the entire house shook. What was this now? An earthquake?

No, it was machine-like, familiar: the rotor and blades of a helicopter. People hurried to the windows.

Out on the front lawn, heads whirled and jerked upward to watch a giant red chopper with a yellow logo on its side for APM EXPORTERS circle over Poplar Avenue and land on a hastily-vacated patch of empty yard on the far edge of the Dunwoody property. Its spinning blades kicked up a small cyclone of snow, and because most witnesses were ducking or looking away, few noticed a short woman wrapped in a down jacket and scarf climb out its side door, followed by a tall, tanned man in his late 50s, wearing dark glasses and an Italian-made fur hat over his graying hair.

The steadicams kept rolling inside as Dave went to the front door and swung it open. The short woman was alone on the steps, and Rashid was keeping her back. She had pulled off her hood to reveal an aging but sweet Latina face, and she gave Dave a heartwarming smile.

"You are my *pequeña bellaza*'s new friend?"

"Well...I'm Dave. Who are—"

"Amanda's oldest friend. And I think she will see me."

Amanda had heard her voice from the other room, and it sizzled through her like that long-gone bacon smell, but this came with memories of morning tamales on the back porch in Chatsworth, of late-night card house building with an occasional shot of Cusha, Cuban salsa playing on the stereo.

"SOFIA!"

She let go of Fran after squeezing her hand, then raced over and caught Sofia in her arms. Dave couldn't believe it; their house really *had* become like a TV sitcom with people coming in the front door. After the women hugged for a good ten seconds, Amanda turned to the hovering camera lens.

"I can't believe she's here!! The best nanny ever in the history of nannies!"

"Don't tell me," said Dana, who hurried over, "Aunt Sophie in Arcadia, right?"

"Yeah. As if! Like everything else I was supposed to say. Thanks to that witch in there!"

Steadicam-2 swung around and zoomed in on Myra, slowly rising to her feet, gravy dripping off her skirt and staring icy laser daggers at Sofia.

"How did you get here...You were deported!"

"*Si.* I was," said Sofia defiantly, turning to the riveted crowd, "By this same witch. She call INS on me one day before Miss Amanda sang for school in Ojai."

"She's lying! I just happened to be there to take the poor orphaned girl in. She never would have had her wonderful career without my help!"

"BULLSHIT!" screamed Amanda, "Sofia taught me to sing and dance for two years! We were best friends and you took her away from me?? You're *worse* than a witch!"

Myra huffed and sputtered and grimaced, and couldn't decide whether to stay in the shadows or step out of them.

"She can't prove it. And even if I did, how the hell did she get back in?"

"I can answer both of those questions."

It was a male voice, soft but assured, coming from the tall, graying man coming through the front door behind Sofia. Amanda recognized the voice a moment before their eyes met, and nearly popped from their sockets.

"Oh my cripes...I knew you put up that reward. I KNEW IT!"

The man removed his fur hat and dark glasses. Amanda melted, rushed up and embraced him too. Myra looked faint.

"It wasn't Rondo Moroni at all," she said, pointing a long fingernail at him, "It was YOU!!"

The man nodded and looked right into the camera with a resigned smile.

"Alan Mushnik. It's nice to meet you all, and to see my daughter again." He kissed Amanda's forehead and the two of them began to sob. So did half the crew and perhaps half of the world. Amwolf just looked at his watch, held up a hand...

"And...CUT, bitte!"

* * *

Cookie Calhoun came marching up to Poplar Avenue minutes later, and was met by a delirious Lakota and Heather as she neared the commotion-filled front yard. The Little Monsters were holding up their phones.

"Normandie's dad just flew in!"

"Did you see that 'Fran Dunwoody' is trending?"

"And 'Fran & Amanda' is now a hashtag?"

"It's amazing!!"

"Not for long," said Cookie with a cold expression, and kept walking toward the house with a hand stuffed in her parka pocket.

"What the hell are you doing?" asked Lakota, and Cookie suddenly whipped out the Glock 27 pistol she proudly kept in its holster on her bedroom closet door beside the L.L. Bean orange hunting vest she had ordered online and had yet to use.

"Normandie's loser dad, huh? Good. He must be the one with the reward money, and I'm gonna freakin' get it from him."

"No!!" yelled Lakota and Cookie shoved her in the snow, kept walking. Rashid saw her coming but wasn't armed and put up his hands. People began to scatter. Cookie stopped a few feet from the steps and raised the gun at Rashid.

"Get out here, Mr. Vine!!"

No one breathed for a few seconds. Then Monty Matilda lunged through the air and knocked Cookie into the snow. Dropped on top of her and squeezed her wrist until the weapon slipped from her hand. Cookie looked up at his curly ginger hair, rough, powerful face and piercing blue eyes and her expression miraculously softened.

"Well, hello luv," said Monty.

"Hi," said Cookie.

* * *

Alan Mushnik of Alan P. Mushnik Exporters, with offices in New York, Chicago, and Milan, stayed in the Dunwoody house for hours after the crew had packed up and left, the media and equipment trucks had left, and Meg Strump had safely reclaimed her front yard without stabbing anyone.

He sat with Sofia and the Dunwoodys at the hastily re-assembled dining table, enjoying a turkey and stuffing sandwich made by Trish and a glass of red wine.

"I hope you can understand. All these years...all I've ever wanted to do was apologize to Amanda."

"Today's been a pretty good start, Dad," said Amanda. Her father set his wine glass down to clutch her hand.

Like the others in the room, Dave found himself completely engaged in Alan's story—maybe even more so. Trying to help his drug-addicted wife while raising emotional, spunky Amanda had just been too much for Alan, and after Amanda's mom drove into that tree things got far more overwhelming in a hurry.

"Sofia was a godsend, without question the best nanny I ever hired, someone who was sweet and gracious and a wonderful Guatemalan cook." Sofia blew him a kiss from across the table. "Most important, she was a very close friend for Amanda."

"Well yeah. Who else did I have? I mean, you weren't there—"

"I know, I know. Just call me the wealthiest deadbeat of all time."

"Sure, I can do that." They shared a little smile to keep the atmosphere light.

It was certainly painful for Alan to leave his daughter in Sofia's care, but new opportunities for his business had opened up in Europe and it just seemed like the arrangement could work. His letters and emails and occasional overseas calls with Amanda began to dwindle, and he hated himself for that, but he was happy to hear she was singing and writing songs and doing so damn well with Sofia that by the time he met his first Italian wife, it was easier for Alan to be even less in touch with his daughter.

He was angry when he heard Sofia had been sent back to Las Morenas, but his business was just beginning to boom, and Amanda had recently been discovered by a very successful talent manager. Myra Harp had seen her perform at an Ojai high school musical competition and had even put her up in the guest house behind her Pacific Palisades home.

Two years later, his daughter had been re-named Normandie Vine and was seizing the pop world. Alan watched and admired and felt proud of her from afar, but when her troubles began and finally peaked in the Colorado mountains, he knew it was time to pull some of his long-accumulated and productive government strings.

* * *

After Mr. Mushnik finished his meal most of them repaired to the den. Fran found herself standing next to Amanda, red-faced and without the power of speech.

"Don't tell me," said Amanda, "You feel awkward about what happened during dinner."

"Well, yeah. Especially because I'd never done anything like that in my life. Not even with a girl at school—"

"Don't be embarassed. It was an honest moment. A real feeling. And believe me, those things kick ass every time."

"Yeah, but...I probably shouldn't have—"

"Slipped me tongue? Not exactly my thing, but it was pretty good technique." Fran managed to give Normandie a teary grin and quick, non-kissing embrace.

Minutes later, Normandie had joined Sofia on the couch. Trish sat on its arm, staring endearingly at their new good friend and favorite nanny-in-law. Dave was nearby discussing imported veterinary supplies with Mr. Mushnik.

"I was as happy for your success as your mother would have been," said Sofia, patting Amanda's hand.

"Well," said Amanda, "Don't think I ever would've blasted off without your rocket fuel. What was that song called that we danced to every night?"

" 'Conga'!" cried Sofia. Fran snapped a finger and yanked out her phone.

"Come in, Spotify..."

In less than a minute, Gloria Estefan and the Miami Sound Machine's "Conga" was blasting out of Fran's phone, and Amanda and Sofia were gloriously doing the salsa again. Fran and Trish joined in immediately, and after much hesitation, Alan Mushnick and even Dave Dunwoody moved their knees to the beat.

* * *

Hours earlier, Paul Stein had ushered a stricken Myra back into their town car for the long ride back to the Omaha airport. Reporters hounded them via phone, TV helicopter and adjacent freeway lane the entire way, and when they reached the airport, Nebraska state police were waiting, having been alerted by state police from Colorado and Utah who had some questions to ask. Sure, *Pre-Thanksgiving with Normandie* probably set some kind of reality show ratings record, but for the first time, Myra wasn't even thinking about that.

EPILOGUE: KALE SHAKES

It was a year and six months later. May was nearly everyone's favorite month in town, when the cottonwoods bloomed, actual green grass took over Endeavor Square, and Googy's sponsored the Southern Central Nebraska Soap Box Derby that began atop the Main Street hill and crossed its finish line in the supermarket parking lot.

May was also graduation time, and Trish was one of nineteen seniors doing their red and yellow-gowned walk in the school auditorium on a gorgeous Friday afternoon. She had been accepted at the University of North Texas College of Music for the fall, and was already packing her first bag.

"Forget the dumb cap," said Fran in the school bathroom as she struggled to pin it on her sister's freshly permed hair.

"I can't do that," said Trish, "Want me to be the only person without one?"

"Yeah. Live a little for once."

She finally got the cap to stay with the help of a third pin, and the girls rushed down the hall to the ceremony, Trish's robe flapping behind her. Dave was just arriving himself from the clinic after uneventfully putting Caleb Souza's favorite old chicken to sleep. He still had his white doctor coat on. Dana, who would graduate the following year, was shooting video of the event with two cameras, one that would produce a black-and-white Expressionist version. All of the formerly known Cookie Monsters were on hand except Cookie herself, who had eloped with Monty Matilda to Australia the previous spring and was currently bored out of her wits in their Melbourne apartment waiting for him to return from shooting some celebrity honeymoon on Kauai.

The graduation itself was short and very routine, the way Endeavorites preferred things. It had taken nearly a month after the forever known "Pre-Thanksgiving Invasion" for the last of the annoying reporters to finally disappear from town. By that time, a freak snowstorm in Los Angeles on the day of the Academy Awards had sent nearly every entertainment wag and paparazzi fleeing to Hollywood for some shiny new over-saturation. Myra Harp, who had retired from celebrity management to open a TV commercial casting office, skidded off the road in Benedict Canyon while speeding to the awards to try and get her name on the complimentary ticket list—and putting her even more out of commission.

Fran watched the graduation beside her new friend Emma Liss. Emma was a freckled, first-year cutie who moved to Endeavor from way up in Hay Springs, and the two of them were openly holding hands within weeks. The last year had seen so many changes in Fran's life, and unflinching courage on her part was certainly the biggest.

"So can you make the after-party?" she whispered to Emma halfway through the diploma call of nineteen names.

"You bet!" said Emma, stroking Fran's arm.

Throughout the auditorium, the very same question was being asked by nearly every student, so it was no surprise an hour later after a bake sale and fruit punch in the cafeteria put on by the school, that a caravan of vehicles and bicycles rolled two miles up Route 79-A to Amanda's Wagon Wheel Sing 'n' Fling Lodge.

Amanda had made good on her live TV promise to retire from famous life. Various contract issues needed to be resolved, of course, but along with Alan Mushnik's help, she had a small batallion of attorneys to make that happen. Then it was merely a matter of pouring some of her extensive earnings into the Wagon Wheel when Elsa Blue Lake passed away the previous summer and the property became available. Amanda had never been a boda fide small town girl, but she was one in heart and spirit, and Endeavor turned out to be a perfect place where she could put her face to the sweet prairie winds and eventually be left alone. The Wagon Wheel became a combination motel/veggie café/art and recording studio Trish and Fran visited routinely, and after Amanda helped Dave at his clinic for a few months until he could find a new full-time assistant, the place also was advertised as pet-friendly. There had been a handful of "Where is Normandie now?" pieces in *People* and *Rolling Stone* and a few on the national evening news, but they dwindled and vanished before long.

Over the summer she'd be taking the Dunwoodys to Tuscany for a few weeks to stay at her father's villa—a trip Dave was already anxious about for flying reasons—but on this gorgeous Friday, that was still a ways ahead of them. A small stage had been set up in the middle of the rented cabin circle, and a modest little country combo from Topeka Amanda had contacted played Hank Williams and Patsy Cline songs while Amanda and Trish sang some duets and Dave rocked on his heels. Cliff and Jean would live inside him always, like warm table lamps seen through curtains on a chilly evening, and he was starting to realize he could be happy with that.

Vegan burgers were barbequed, wine, beer, and kale shakes were served, and a good time was had by dozens. The sun bid farewell after dinner and a planetarium of stars replaced it. Fran and Emma happily twirled under them, whispering in each other's ears, while Dave and Amanda rekindled their friendly waltz, and all was right and promising under the big Nebraska sky.

ABOUT THE AUTHOR

 JEFF POLMAN is a former newspaper journalist and produced screenwriter who now contributes to the *Huffington Post* and other Web sites. He has published four historical baseball novels, and *The Invasion of Normandie* is his first foray into non-horsehide fiction. Originally from New England, he resides in Culver City, CA.

Web: jeffpolman.com
Twitter: @jpballnut